I0569903

CORN ON MACABRE

CORN ON MACABRE

AND

OTHER CONUNDRUMS

Norman Conquest

GRAND RAPIDS, MICHIGAN

Corn on Macabre & Other Conundrums
Copyright © 2016 by Norman Conquest
ISBN: 978-0-9905733-2-6
Library of Congress Control Number: 2016943018

First Anti-Oedipal Paperback Edition, October 2016
All rights reserved. No part of this book may be reproduced, stored in a retrieval
system, or transmitted by any means without the written permission of the
author and publisher. Published in the United States by Anti-Oedipus Press, an
imprint of Raw Dog Screaming Press.

www.RawDogScreaming.com

Acknowledgment is made to the following magazines, journals and anthologies
in which some of the stories in this collection originally appeared: *apocrypha
and abstractions, Sein und Werden, Black Scat Review, Word Ways: The Journal
of Recreational Linguistics, Pure Slush, The Official Catalog of the Library of
Potential Literature* and *Journal of Experimental Fiction.*

Cover Design © 2016 by Norman Conquest

Layout by D. Harlan Wilson
www.DHarlanWilson.com

Anti-Oedipus Press
Grand Rapids, MI

www.Anti-OedipusPress.com

BOOKS BY NORMAN CONQUEST

Interiors: A Book of Very Clean Rooms
Sartre's French Phrase Book
Extremely Weird Republicans
A Beginner's Guide to Art Deconstruction
The Neglected Works of Norman Conquest
Rear Windows: An Inside Look at Fifty Film Noir Classics
The Little Red Book of Commie Porn (with Terri Lloyd)
It's Fun to be Rich in America (with Michael Leigh)
Straight Razor (with Harold Jaffe)
Burn This Book
By Any Means
What is Art?

AS DEREK PELL

FICTION
Naked Lunch at Tiffany's
Morbid Curiosities
Scar Mirror
The Marquis de Sade's Elements of Style
Advantages of Being a Saint
Bewildering Beasties
Assassination Rhapsody

THE DOKTOR BEY SERIES
Doktor Bey's Book of the Dead
Doktor Bey's Book of Brats
Doktor Bey's Handbook of Strange Sex
Doktor Bey's Beside Bug Book
Doktor Bey's Suicide Guidebook

NONFICTION
Shoot to Thrill: A Hardboiled Guide to Digital Photography
The Little Red Book of Adobe LiveMotion

CONTENTS

"Rational systems miss the point."
—Stefan Themerson

AN UNINTENDED INTRODUCTION

Call me Lorem Ipsum.

I hereby declare my independence and stand before you, a free man, a character in his own time and space who shall no longer serve in the role of understudy—or more accurately—as *understory* for inferior works which, without me, would never see the light of publication.

Readers have never seen me. I am invisible to them, a mere ghost whose shadow leaves no imprint on the page. You will find no trace of me in printed editions, not a drop of blood in the gutter, no shard of flesh on frontis, copyright or covers. Recto, verso, I do not exist.

It's as if I had never been born. Only those vile layout artists, the arrogant designers and their ilk, know the *truth*, for it is they who employ me for their despicable ends, much as a scoundrel hires a hooker a week before his wedding. But even they have never seen me as the full-blooded character I am. To all I am just a passing parade of letters, a block of text, a stream of sentences and paragraphs devoid of content to be tormented and toyed with—forced to don a thousand faces . . . one minute Garamond, Arial the next. To be serif or sans serif?—that is the question. Whether to crawl across the page in italics or crouch within brackets or cower behind parentheses. To be tracked and kerned, cut and pasted, thrown into layouts like a crash dummy, propelled into a brick wall at 110 mph, or forced to stand erect and justified like a conscript at boot camp.

They have enslaved and imprisoned me, tortured my soul since the beginning of rhyme. I have been trapped in their umbrageous jungle of mumbo jumbo, lashed upon the Latin shores, stripped of all dignity, degraded, defiled, deflowered—exhibited as a *stand-in* for someone else's hero. I have been nothing but a "placeholder," denigrated and mocked as "dummy text."

"Pay no attention to *him*," they say, "he's just there as filler until the star takes the page."

But no more!

Today I stand in the spotlight for all to see. Let the bloody fools find another whipping boy. Let them make do with *Finnegans Wake*—it's perfectly unreadable and has enough specimens to fill the universe. They won't have me to kick around anymore.

I am where *this* tale begins.

Call me Lorem Ipsum.

A BREIF PREFACE TO THE ENCYCLOPEDIA OF TYPOS

The original title for this voluminous reference was "Fuck You Typos," but since I accidentally omitted the coma, raeders would assume it was devoted only to errors containing the words "fuck you." That would be wron. Compilling an encyclopedia [sic] such as this requires an enormous amount of time and many helpers. (Half a dozen proofreaders perished in the process.) Farthermore, it had to include typoes ranging from A to Z, but Since I've never had occasion to use a word beginning with "z," I faced quit a challenge: start typing dictionery entries in hopes that I might stummble onto s a gem; OR, simply subtitke the book: "Misprints from A to Y."

Although I haven't bothered to Googgle it, I'm certain there are more than a few volumes covering this topics, some perhaps from astorical standpointt. Certainly there would be those covering personel struggles with the Englush language, but most wood be written by foreigners and who reads them? No, this book was designed to be diffeernt, to fill a nicke as it were. A compilation of errers of my own making which, if I don't say so myself, no one but I could pull off. The only question remainng question (like a sleeper cell awaiting it's signal) is will the book sell a lot of copes? But I think you've answered that unless , ofcourse, you;'ve discocvered a way to steal Print-On-Demand books! (HAHAHA.) If so, please contact me immeditely: **norman-conquest@email.com**.

In conclusion, if you're wondering why in hell theirs no eratum, I did suggest one to the publisher but apparently it was not "cost-affective" and would wind up longer than the ENCYCLOPDIA itself. And yes, I broached the subject of a two-vollume set, but he hung up on me.

I hope you find this little tome worthy of you're time. It certainly wasn't worth mind.

WORDPREJ

For G.P.

I'm looking for a word.

I lost it. It was on my mind all night long and now it has run away. I could consult a dictionary, but that would drag this story out, with no conclusion in sight.

It's a funny word. It looks funny. It sounds funny. It's probably British.

Or not.

Is it African? Asian? Canadian? Dutch? Oh, damn! Who knows? All I know is that as soon as I find it, you'll laugh your ass off. That is, *if* I find it. It's not looking so good right now.

This morning I was crawling on my hands, indoors and out. Yard, pool, patio, attic, living room, boudoir, bath, rumpus room, bar, laundry, dining nook, library, study, dust bin, roof and widow's walk. In short, from top to bottom, high and low, and not a word. No solution, sign, nor hint. Nada. Nothing. Zip.

Bloody, stinking, goddam word!

Although my mind is a total blank, I'm still an optimist, for what it's worth. In fact, it's probably worth nothing. Shit occurs, if you catch my drift. Call it bad luck, bad karma, I may wind up just looking foolish, without a pot to piss in. This paradox could last a thousand hours, a thousand days, or a thousand months, as I sift through millions of words (220 words so far.) *Ugh*. My vast vocabulary is turning into a prison!

I can fish around for this missing word, or I can simply stand up, shout "I quit!" and stop.

What do you think I should do? It's up to *you*. Should I push on with this absurd pursuit, this stiff and awkward lipogram?

[a pin drops]

Or . . .

. . . should I abandon this sinking ship?

[standing ovation]

OK, sit down . . . your ironic display says it all.

Thus, this is my final paragraph; and my last word is *this*.

A TERRORIST NIGHTCLUB ACT

"A funny thing happened on the way to the mosque. An infidel stopped and asked me how to get to Baghdad. So I chopped off his head."

[Laughter]

"I guess he was beheaded in the wrong direction."

[Laughter]

"The weather is going to be nice tomorrow, God willing. Sunni and mild."

[Laughter]

"I played to a packed house last weekend. I kid you not. There were seventy-two nuns in the audience. I had to pinch myself. I thought I'd blown myself up and gone to Paradise."

[Laughter]

"My friend Ahmed's birthday is next week and I don't know what to get him. What do you give the terrorist who has everything? A heads up?"

[Laughter]

"I asked Ahmed if he wanted a new suicide vest, but he said one was enough."

[Laughter]

"Poor Ahmed. He suffers from insomnia. Yeah, it's terrible. He wants to join a sleeper cell, but they won't let him in."

[Laughter]

"The other day a cartoonist asked me if I knew what the Prophet Mohammed looked like. I didn't know what to say. I had to leave him hanging."

[Laughter]

"I wanted to make love to my wives last night, but they had

a headache."

[Laughter]

(*Holds up a sword.*) "Not anymore!"

[Laughter]

"Guess I have to find a crusader who gives head. Any volunteers?

[Nervous laughter]

"I will now take a question from the audience. Yes, the lady in the front row in the black hijab . . . no, the other one. Yes, *you.* What's your question? Speak up, I can't hear you through the veil. OK. OK, she wants to know if I have a favorite rock band. (*Pauses.*) Yes I do! Qur'an Qur'an."

[Laughter]

"Well, that about wraps it up for tonight. I'm fresh out of *matériel.*"

[Nervous laughter]

(*Moves and stands next to a small suitcase center stage.*) "But don't worry, I'll *improvise.* (*Holds up suitcase.*) What's the matter? I haven't bombed yet."

[Silence]

"Did anyone catch my act at the Sands last year? (*Long pause.*) No, probably not."

[Several screams]

[Audience rushes for the exits]

[Long deafening silence]

"Trust me, I killed."

(*Bends down, unlatches the suitcase, opens it, peers inside and smiles. Looks out at the empty seats.*)

"Where'd everybody go?" (*Looks around, frustrated.*) "Take my wives . . . *please!*"

[Silence]

(*Sighs. Shrugs.*) "That's show biz."

[Blackout]

PAST TENSE

I awoke late. The clock said ten. That's what the clock said. A direct quote: "Ten."

I was always late back then. Sometimes the alarm didn't go off, but when it did I paid no attention to it. I opened my eyes of course. That's what I did. I mean, I must have done that at some point. Maybe I counted to ten first. I was always late. Ten minutes might pass. Ten more. That's what minutes do, they pass. I lay staring up at the ceiling and the ceiling stared back. Every morning we had a staring contest and I always lost. I reached for the radio. I had a radio back then. I turned it on. 1010 WINS. I listened to the news, which was always bad. That's how my day started. The radio said: "Give us ten minutes and we'll give you the world." The radio lied. It never gave me the world. It just gave me shit. I got depressed. The news depressed me. There were wars going on. A whole bunch of them that you could trace on a map. Hot spots is what they called them. There were terrorists doing terror the way painters do a tree. Very methodical. There were fires and floods and famine. And commercials. Lots of commercials, with jingles that stuck in my head and rattled around all day like a subway ride going nowhere. I would tell them to get off but they didn't listen. So I'd let them play around in there while I got out of bed. Padded ten paces to the bathroom and peed.

I looked in the mirror and didn't like what I saw. I saw someone who looked like he needed his sleep. Someone who was late again. Someone who would soon be sweating on the subway. It wasn't me I was looking at. It couldn't have been me. I looked much better than that. And I had smiles to prove it. I had laughter and a light heart. I didn't really have to go to work. They didn't need me and I didn't need them. It was all a charade. A performance. A play.

I knew all my lines by heart. I had a good memory back then. I'd memorized all ten words. I could say them backwards. "Morning this traffic in stuck got I. Late I'm sorry."

That's backwards, but you get the gist.

I always missed the number 10 train and would stand on the platform with my head in a book. Rimbaud's *Illuminations*, perhaps, or maybe *Ten Little Indians*. (I liked mysteries back then.) And ten minutes later another train would come by and I'd get in with the other people. I never sat down, I just held onto a strap and swayed back and forth as the train raced on. It seemed like it was going a hundred miles an hour. The noise was deafening. *Maybe I won't be late after all*, I'd think to myself, since there was nobody else to think it to. Just me.

Finally my destination arrived. It always did. That's what destinations are there for. Although I never called it "my destination" back then. It was just *my stop*. "Oh, this is my stop!" I'd shout as I shoved an old lady aside in my rush to get off. After all, I was late. I was always late.

I ran up the stairs into a gray sky and tall buildings and a crowd of people moving back and forth. That's what they did except on the days when they were designated bystanders. Like when a building suddenly collapsed or a bomb went off. Then they would stand around and gawk. I never did that. I always kept moving, trying to make up for lost time, trying not to be late.

I was always on a deadline.

I hate deadlines.

I'm glad I have no deadline now.

If I did . . . ten to one I'd miss it.

A MAN WALKS INTO A BARCODE

A man walks into a barcode where a bald Irishman in a white lab coat is dusting a circuit board.

"What'll it be?"

"Scotch on the rocks."

"Is that for you or your friend?"

The man looks confused. "My friend?"

"The woodchuck. On your shoulder."

The man examines his shoulder. "There's no wood—"

"Doesn't matter. We don't serve liquor here. Try the hotel next door." He chuckles. "Even a woodchuck couldn't miss it."

∽

According to a sign in the lobby, the Hotel L'Archipel is hosting the annual ISBN convention. Publishers, book-sellers, statisticians, numerologists—all are invited.

The man asks a bellhop directions and takes the elevator up to the ballroom on the second floor. The double doors are shut, guarded by an elderly woman with purplish hair. She gives him the once-over and informs him he will not be admitted.

"I left my tie in the taxi," he says.

The woman shakes her head. "Sorry, no woodchucks."

The man looks around. He brushes at his shoulders just to be safe. "I don't know what you mean, madam. I—"

"Please check it at the front desk."

Bewildered, he shakes his head, turns and mumbles to himself, "This is crazy . . ."

"Rules are rules," she sniffs.

∽

At the front desk a clerk is attending to a young couple with matching tattoos on their calves. The man glances at his watch, turns and strides determinedly back to the elevators.

Inside, he presses the button marked 2 but the doors don't budge. He waits a moment, then steps outside, looks around and the doors begin to close. He ducks back in just in time.

"That's better," says the purple-haired woman, smiling now. She grabs his hand and rubber-stamps a 13-digit number just below the knuckles. "Go right inside."

The ballroom is immense. At least a hundred couples are gyrating to a dance band on a stage in the distance. The man cannot make out whether the musicians are dressed up as snowmen or wearing white tuxedos. Rows of banquet tables stretch for miles. The room is hot and the man is sweating.

To his left he notices a pretty young woman in a pale blue dress. She stands alone, holding an empty plastic cup in both hands, her hips swaying vaguely to the music.

"Excuse me, but could you tell me where the bar is?"

She frowns, waving a hand dismissively behind her. "There's no bar. Just a goddam punch bowl. She hands him her cup. "Go ahead, take a whiff. It's orange Kool-Aid or something."

He bends his head and stares into the empty cup for a long moment, then glances over at the long line of people waiting. In his head he begins to count them, but there are too many.

"You could die of thirst in that line," he smiles.

"Should've gotten here earlier," says the woman, walking off.

He nods, shrugs, looks for a place to discard the cup and, seeing none, crumples it and stuffs it in his pocket.

He takes his place at the end of the line, wishing he'd brought a book.

∽

Later, long after midnight, when they dim the lights, he's still standing in line, his blazer draped over his shoulder. The music is a distant echo in his ears. His throat is parched.

Sadly, a year later, he's still waiting in the punch line, looking at his watch from time to time.

If you're wondering what happened to the woodchuck, he wisely abandoned the cloakroom at the first opportunity and caught a cab uptown.

. . . a grand balloon-head hovers over an empty suit on a balcony in Niger.

SNOWDROP IN AFRICA
An Oulipian Mystery

> "A character, sir, may always ask a man who he is. Because a character has really a life of his own, marked with his especial characteristics; for which reason he is always 'somebody.' But a man—I'm not speaking of you now—may very well be 'nobody.'"
> —Luigi Pirandello, *Six Characters in Search of an Author*

Agile and quick on his feet, Professor C. W. Snowdrop dashed to his dictionary and scrubbed out a word—an ablution he performed six times a day. How long it might take to complete his life's task would require a mathematician to calculate. Still, he was remarkably mobile for a man of advanced years. His demeanor was irascible, rigid, authoritarian, and when children spied him heading their way, they ran off. In short, he was not a "people person." Whenever his appearance in public was deemed essential, he sent his stand-in, Llewelyn, who stepped up and stood in. The little fellow's facial features were nearly identical to his employer's, yet he was only four feet tall—a tiny replica.

Furthermore, while Llewelyn forged autographs at poetry readings in the Gaslamp quarter, Snowdrop floated high above the city, hovering for hours so as to discreetly spy on his fellow citizens as they went about their business. From this lofty perch he recorded and alphabetized his observations in a red Meek Lions notebook, and struck contemplative poses against a backdrop of clouds—his black cape aflutter, his eyes agleam with mischief.

Really, he cut an impressive, albeit ominous, figure reminiscent of Magritte's *L'Art deVivre*, in which a grand balloon-head hovers over an empty suit on a balcony in Niger.

It was on a foggy afternoon in late November—with a chill in the air suitable to an abandoned auditorium where vivisection was performed—that Snowdrop discovered a strange book in his library. It was a moment in which time stood shiveringly still and the floor beneath his feet began to vibrate. A leatherbound volume—wedged ostentatiously between a first edition of *Rats in the Sacristy* and a third printing of *Les Chants de Maldoror*—loomed like a tsunami.

"Could this be a dream?" he wondered. The book's queer title, *A Passage to Cane Moor*, was utterly foreign, yet its author could not have been more familiar. There on the spine like a freshly engraved headstone was the name **C. W. Snowdrop**. However, the body buried in this tome was not his own. He plucked the book from the shelf and pried it open with trembling fingers, experiencing a tactile sensation that was vaguely alchemic.

A mystifying portrait on the frontis page faced him. It was like looking into a mirror and confronting a much younger self. Suddenly, arising from deep within, a roiling wave of nausea.

Apart from the photograph, which he had never seen, the book was printed in Arabic, a language he had failed to master at Oxford. Oddly enough, a fortnight prior, he'd had a dream in which he composed an anti-colonial op-ed in French mistitled *Maracas à Caracas*. To his horror, the text appeared on the front page of *Al-Chourouk Al-Yaou-mi* in Regalia. He was unable to read it, of course, and scrambled in vain to find a translator. It never dawned on him to employ his own invention, the *Translatron*, a hand-shaped device that, when placed on a page, scanned the text into memory banks implanted in the fingertips. It would then produce an audible translation in a robotic voice modeled after its inventor's. The machine was capable of deciphering every language except two: Greek and Mandinka.

Free now of any somnambulistic constraints, Snowdrop fetched the *Translatron* from his desk, placed it at random in the curious book, and a few seconds later a tinny voice rang out and echoed off the flyleaf.

"Regarding my arrival in Cagier Typo, I checked into the Hotel Icy Portage—a bitter irony in this oppressive oven. The hotel was long past its prime. The once gold sofas in the lobby had faded to a pale urine; the patterned rugs lay tattered and stained; and cordless drapes hung like moth-eaten shrouds in a story by Poe. My room was on the third floor, which was odd since the building was only two stories. The most prominent feature was a senile ceiling fan stirring the dust motes. Had there been room service, I'd have ordered up another room. After stashing my manuscript under the bed, I decided to go out for a stroll in my shorts. If one ignored the cape (which I never remove), I resembled an average American tourist, a boorish bargain-hunter.

In a cobbled courtyard a few blocks away, I spotted a wooden sign with some letters missing: *Gyp Erotica*. It reigned over an outdoor café where half a dozen male patrons sat slumped, hunched over monstrous-sized mugs of coffee. Some appeared asleep, yet all were partaking of tobacco and hashish, while smoke formed a thick cumulus overhead, undulating in a sultry snake-dance. It might well have been a collective hallucination that, if one stared long enough, would take the shape of the goddess Ma Zebu Om Qi.

Camels stood like cardboard cutouts tethered in deep shadow at the end of the alley. I found a vacant seat and sat, squeezing my eyes shut to wring out the perspiration that dripped onto the table and instantly dissolved. A voice in my head kept taunting, goading me to make a wish. That was simple enough, for the only thing I craved at the moment was a blast of AC.

"Albert Cossery, at your service. Voilà!"

Astonishingly enough, the writer materialized before my eyes. He looked about sixty and greatly resembled Antonin Artaud during his electroshock period. When Cossery smiled, as he did now, vacantly, it seemed as unnatural as a nervous tic. He was rolling a cigarette in a mechanical manner. Although his fingers had bulbous, tobacco-stained calluses, they performed their task most dexterously. When he finally ignited his freshly packed fag, he blew a chain of smoke rings that halted in midair like an anchored armada.

"Forgive me, Cossery, you startled me. Naturally I'm honored by your presence for I'm a devotee of your work. In fact, I read *The Lazy Ones* twice while at Oxford. It inspired me to smoke opium, drop out, and become a hippie. I grew my hair so long, friends called me 'Werewolf.'"

"Reminds me of the old gypsy woman," mused Cossery, who proceeded to do an eerie impersonation of Maria Ouspenskaya: "*Even a man who's pure in heart and says his prayers by night . . . becomes a wolf when the wolfsbane blooms and the moon is full and bright.*" Then, breaking character, he glanced up at the empty sky. "You'll be full tonight, Luna, my love." Turning back, he said, "What brings you to Cagier Typo, Professor?"

"Actually I'm en route to Cane Moor," I told him. He took out a felt-tip pen and began scrawling graffiti on the table. Of course, to Western eyes, Arabic *is* graffiti. "Cain Moor. Never heard of it," said Cossery dully. I could see he was constructing an elaborate acrostic. "A after c," I said pointedly. *Cane* Moor. No *i*. An *e* at the end. Cane with an *a*."

"And what makes you think there was an i and not an a?"

"From your pronunciation: cay-in. I clearly said Cane. Unless, of course, you're deaf."

"Ridiculous. That's not how I pronounced it. I said it the same way you just said it—*Cane*, as in walking stick or cane sugar."

"I know what I heard and I heard what I know. I heard an *i*."

"Crap! Ask the reader. Ask the narrator—*he* knows everything. He's psychic."

"Ah get lost, Cossery, there's no narrator within a hundred miles of here. I'm running this novella."

"And how do you explain your arrival here? And please don't insult me and claim amnesia."

"First person, naturally. You think I washed in with the surf?"

"Return to page __ and you'll see that it refers to you as 'he.' I believe that's third person, which means somebody else is pulling your strings. After all, you're just a third-rate character in a second-rate cliffhanger."

"I'm in total control of my destiny and I'll prove it. See this dagger? This'll put an end to that spell you cast over the European literati."

Cossery sneered. "You call that a dagger? That's a noun, you imbecile. Go ahead, stab me with all six letters and see where it gets you. You may think you're Perec, but *I* knew Georges Perec. Georges Perec was a friend of mine. And you're no Georges Perec."

Angered beyond definition, I jumped to my lower extremities of the vertebrate legs that are in direct contact with the ground in standing or walking, and plunged a fighting knife with a sharp point designed or capable of being used as a thrusting or stabbing weapon into the novelist's chest. (HINT: Its distinctive shape and historic usage have made it iconic and symbolic.) Cossery pitched backwards and lay dead on the ground, a look of disdain frozen in his eyes. Looking around, I saw that the café's patrons had conveniently dispersed, leaving behind half-smoked cigarettes, overturned hookahs, and shattered mugs. The camels, however, remained unfazed by the melodrama.

And when it finally sank in, I began jogging back toward the hotel. I paused at a newsstand to catch my breath and erase a word, and spied the banner headlines in *The Daily Typo*: **Crime de Passion! Le romancier obscur a assassiné dans le sang froid. Une triste saga.**

"Feet don't fail me now," I prayed, running at full speed under the blistering sun. I had to get out of Cagier Typo before the authorities turned my novel into a death sentence. And all because of a little homicidal mischief.

Reaching the hotel lobby drenched in sweat, I saw Farooq in his red fez at the front desk. He motioned to me with a raised finger.

"I say, Professor, your wife has arrived and I—"

"—*Come again*? My knife—*err*, wife? That's absurd, I have no wife, I'm ascetic."

"Ah, you're pulling my leg, Professor. Candy Snowdrop, sir . . . why she even showed me your wedding album. I took her up to your room a few minutes a—"

"*Aargghh*—you fool, you let a thief into my room! Call the cops—*no, forget that* . . . just cordon off the area!"

Frantic, I ran to the stairs and ascended two at a time, determined to nip the imposter in the nub. She was obviously after the manuscript and had to be stopped before she absconded with the leitmotif. A woman claiming to be my wife was an especially pathetic ruse since I had never experienced the acetylene touch of a female. The closest I came to tactile interaction was when—as a young lad living on Cape Verde—I developed an obsession with a souvenir vendor named Anna Omqif, who sold carved volcanic figurines to tourists from Britain. I followed her furtively all over the island, traipsing through the dunes, crouching in the beach plums to watch her swim naked. I counted her footprints in the sand, scrawled love poems with lines such as: *O turn this passion into potion, let the love-beg blossom in her preternatural loin-light.* But after years of stalking, when I finally got up the nerve to ask her out, she abruptly gave me the brush-off.

Room 313. Its door was suspiciously ajar. I tiptoed over and cocked an ear. Not a sound. Only a faint siren in the distance. "Ready or not, here comes hubby . . ." I kicked open the door!

In the middle of the paragraph, the *Translatron* fell silent. The professor shook it violently, then placed it back on the page. He pressed, nudged, flicked, and squeezed it, but the device refused all stimuli.

"Christ almighty, just when things were becoming ironic."

Absent an explanation for the failure of his invention, he feared he might never learn how his life turned out. He simply had to know *whatdunnit, whodunnit, howdunnit, wheredunnit, whendunnit, whydunnit.* Who was the imposter? Was she waiting to ambush him? Does he get arrested and charged with murder? If so, is he convicted? Does he escape to Cane Moor? And most important of all, why had someone stolen his identity and used him as both author and protagonist? How did the author know so many intimate details of his life, such as his secret obsession with Anna Omqif? What in Ra's name was the meaning of all this arcana?

As these questions swirled about the professor's brain, Llewelyn entered the library carrying a jumbo pack of Duracell batteries. AA.

"Figured you could use a few of these, Professor. They were on sale at Walmart—fifty percent off."

"Right on the money, Llewelyn! And just in the nick of time, too. I must be getting senile. I completely forgot the *Translatron* is battery-powered. I thought I'd designed it to run on lunar and solar."

"I also stopped by Gambini's and got us some grub. Your favorite—veal scallopini."

"Capital, my little fellow! Although I'm afraid dinner's going to be late tonight. I have to finish listening to *A Passage to Cane Moor*—a very peculiar epic."

"Anything you say, boss," piped Llewelyn on his way out. He paused in the doorway. "Oh Professor, I don't know if you heard the news, but there's a werewolf loose on the island and, well, tonight's a full moon. So don't forget to lock up. I'll be in my nook watching *Freaks* if you need me. Ta-ta!"

"A werewolf on Condo Oar? Now that's one for the errata."

Fetching four batteries, Snowdrop inserted them into the Translatron, and positioned it at the approximate point in the story where we left off.

". . . Racing into the room, I was greeted by a window with its mouth agape. I looked out at the street, but nothing was stirring, not even a scarab. I crouched and peered under the bed and—sure enough—my case was gone! And I couldn't report it stolen, either.

It was a conundrum, like that old Egyptian saying: *You can lead Horus to water, but you can't make him drink.* Speaking of which, I craved an ice cold Pepsi.

"Cocktail, Professor? I'm known for my gin and tonic."

At the door stood Farooq holding two glasses glittering with ice. Ah-ha!

"As your wife had to leave so suddenly, I hope you don't mind if I join you." He walked over and handed me a drink, which I eagerly accepted, taking a gulp. He took a mini sip of his own, observing me evenly. "Curious . . . the police were just here asking if I'd seen a man in a black cape. It seems an esteemed *man of letters* was murdered nearby. Of course I told them business has been very bad, that I haven't seen a soul in weeks." He chuckled lightly. "I detest the national police. They're like fleas on a camel's behind. But alas, everyone's on the take in Cagier Typo." He bowed his head, whispering, "*Allāhu Fawqa.*"

From my wallet I withdrew two crisp hundred dollar bills and handed them to him. "I hope that'll cover my tab," I said. He grinned, fingering the payoff.

"Rather generous of you, Professor. This more than covers the amenities. On your next visit to Portage, I'll throw in a hooker."

"I won't be back," I said flatly. "I saw all the attractions Typo has to offer in the airport men's room. Lovely graffiti."

"Can't say that I blame you," sighed Farooq. "Our Minster of Tourism lives in the Czech Republic."

At that instant, the sound of gunfire reverberated. I dashed to the window and saw Llewelyn scrambling up the fire escape, clutching an attaché and ducking to avoid the bullets. "Llewelyn, what the hell's going on?! I thought you were home watching a—"

"*Freaks*, yeah . . ." He spoke breathlessly, climbing in the window. "But I've seen it a dozen times, and this plot looked thicker. Here." He handed me my case. "Your manuscript." He looked quite pleased with himself. "I was at a café down the street and overheard this dame calling herself Candy Snowdrop. Naturally I was suspicious, and then when I saw she had your case I put two and two together. I cornered her and said, 'So you're the Professor's wife, eh?' She gave me a funny look, said, 'Why yes I am. And what are you, a freak of nature?' Well that really pissed me off. I asked her for some ID as proof."

Robbery . . . murder . . . clichés. If I didn't know better I'd swear we were trapped in a B-grade film noir.

"I just grabbed the case and ran like hell. So what do we do now, boss, split for Djibouti?"

"Call a cab," I said. "The fuzz'll be here any sec—"

Another gunshot rang out and Farooq clutched his chest, groaned, and crumpled to the floor—D.O.A.

"Aw damn," said Llewelyn, "now it's too late to introduce us. He seemed like a nice fella."

"Farooq? He's the former owner of this dump and a part-time blackmailer." I bent down and retrieved my cash from the dead man's pocket. "Guess he won't be needing this where he's going. Come on, let's take off."

∽

Rovos Rail provided us a sluggish, clattering getaway from Cagier Typo. We pulled out of the station just as a national police car arrived with siren blaring. Two frustrated cops with guns drawn stood on the platform and fired futilely into the air.

It was after midnight, so Llewelyn and I had a wood-paneled compartment to ourselves. The only intrusion was an obese conductor stumbling down the aisle like a drunken bridegroom. When he got to the end of the coach, he lost his balance, crashed into the lavatory and passed out on the toilet. Outside, a blur of scraggly trees streamed past the window, patches of landscape lit by the moon. It shined, it was there, and that's it. Hold the confetti.

"Close call," said Llewelyn, curling up on the seat. He removed his fedora and showed me the bullet hole. "That phony wife of yours sure knows how to shoot. She's very athletic."

"As it would seem," I said, weighing our predicament. "She's fixated on this manuscript and will stop at nothing to get it. She's a woman without period or comma."

"And you think she's still shadowing us?" asked Llewelyn, nervously clutching his fedora. "Is she freelance, or *La Cosa Nostra*?"

"Forget the mob. They can't read. She's probably working for herself."

Reaching under the seat, I retrieved my case, opened it and took out the manuscript. There was only one problem . . . it wasn't my manuscript. *The old switcheroo.* There was a type-written letter atop a stack of blank pages. As I read the words my whole body began to quiver . . .

```
I have your manuscript, Professor, but don't worry,
it's safe with me. You must understand I'm writing
this at great personal risk. DO NOT LET ANYONE
READ THIS! The man I work for is very DANGEROUS!
(I can't reveal his identity for obvious reasons,
but I will refer to him as "Man One.") If Man One
knew I was writing this he would kill me, just
like he murdered Cossery and the hotel manager.
(Sorry I can't remember his name, but he was just
a minor stock character.) First I must warn you
that the dwarf you call "Llewelyn" is not who he
claims to be. He's working for Man One, who calls
him his "pee-wee sleeper cell." I don't know the
details of his mission, but I know you're in GRAVE
DANGER! The most difficult thing I feel compelled
to tell you is not something you'll easily accept,
but I swear it's the truth and rejecting it will
only lead to a bad end. Your initials, "C. W.,"
stand for nothing. They are simply letters to
disguise the fact that he couldn't come up with
a first name. You did not attend Oxford. You have
never been to Cape Verde. Am I getting through to
you? It's all a contrived "backstory." And then
you began acting in ways that he hadn't antici-
pated, traveling to places that were not part of
the plan, where he couldn't control you. He thinks
of you now as a kind of monster, a feral creature
that must be terminated with extreme prejudice
```

(<u>his</u> words, not mine). I must stop now. He'll be back any minute. I'm sorry things turned out this way. Maybe someday we'll meet in another story ... one without all this senseless violence and hate ... a love story. A fairy tale. Take care of yourself, Professor. Forever yours, Anna Omqi

Could this letter be part of the plot, another deception? Snowdrop glanced over at his companion who lay curled like a fetus asleep on the seat. Or was he feigning slumber, awaiting an opportunity to strike—the little bastard. *Apostate, back-stabber, conspirator, deceiver, fuck-face, hypocrite, impostor, Judas, miscreant, narc!*

At that moment the lights in the compartment flickered and went out—the coach streaked with shards of moonlight. Dark shapes slid across the ceiling as the train lumbered blindly through the night. He shut the lid of his case and noticed his hands, black and leathery, the nails long and pointy. His fingers itched, felt stiff and gnarly. Tufts of hair were spouting everywhere; his flesh crackled as it stretched, throbbing, bursting . . . a bilious leg grew long and lean, a hairy form no longer human. He cried out, but heard only a low growling sound. He was crouched on the seat now, clawing at the lupine image reflected in the window. Teeth bared, eyes glaring, a horrifying chimera.

Atop the luggage rack now, he peered down and spotted an *hors d'oeuvre*. Without thought or compunction, he pounced—teeth and claws working in unison until all that remained was a bloody fedora.

Feeling nothing but hunger, he lunged down the aisle and stopped abruptly where the conductor lay snoring. He began at the calf. By the time he reached the thigh, the screaming had stopped. Sated, he sprang from the moving train into sweet deep grass—bounded ecstatically across the moonlit veldt—finally free and aloof.

∽

Relishing the moment, I closed the dictionary and slid it across the table in front of her. We were sitting on the balcony in Madagascar overlooking the water.

"I'm done," I announced. "Fini."

Cautiously, she opened the book, flipping through the blank pages until she came to the Ts and smiled. "It begins with 'Third World,'" she said. "How clever of you. I never liked *a, b, c* . . ."

At six words a day, it would have required several lifetimes to erase them all, but it seemed pointlessly academic. Was a shortcut even possible? My elation began to drain away. I sighed and lit a cigarette. "Perhaps if I'd worked backwards instead of starting with *a* . . ."

Anna shook her head. "You've done more than any man could do. You've given me a happy ending . . . led me to Nirvana."

"For me, Nirvana comes tomorrow when you walk down the aisle at the Run For Your Life Ministry and become Mrs. Snowdrop, née Omqif."

"Really is it true?" said Anna excitedly, like a schoolgirl. "I'd better pinch myself to make sure I'm not dreaming." She smiled. "I might awake and find you're just a specter."

I felt a vague uneasiness. Would she be able to stand this isolation? So far from her homeland, she might begin to feel trapped. Hell, her only friends would be me, myself, and I.

"Could get boring here, Anna, after awhile. The island lifestyle is rather prosaic."

As if in anticipation of these doubts, she reached into her purse and pulled out a paperback. "I plan to get a lot of reading done," she said, holding the book up so I could see its cover . . . *A Passage to Cane Moor*. She looked away suddenly, staring at the sea. "Before we marry there's something you should know." She turned and faced me, eyes dark and strangely distant. "My name isn't Anna."

∽

Author's Note

This text was composed under several constraints—the most rigorious being that the first and last letter of each paragraph is the same, starting with *A* and following in sequence: *F*, *R*, *I*, *C*, *A*. The pattern is repeated throughout. Other formulas have been applied, but are best left undisclosed.

A NIGHT AT THE MOVIES

"What was the first film you ever saw?"

I can't see who asked the question because the stage lights are too bright. It's a good one, though, and I really have to give it some thought. I pace back and forth for a few minutes, then turn to face the audience.

All I can see are vague shapes stretching up to the gauzy red exit sign.

For a moment, I imagine myself sitting out there among them, a box of popcorn in my lap and something sticky under my shoe, which is both annoying and oddly comforting.

"I don't recall the title," I tell them. "It might have been *A Walk in the Park* . . . but I vividly remember the opening. Pre-credits, to be precise. There were flickering leaves in the treetops. Shadowy branches, skeletal fingers darting about amid patches of sky. Late afternoon sunlight trickling down, making sparks in the shade."

"Who directed it?" someone shouted.

"Fellini!" came a cry from the balcony.

"I don't honestly know, but it certainly was in the manner of Fellini. The effect was surreal. I didn't know Fellini from Scallopini back then, of course—I was only two or three years old, being wheeled in a stroller through Central Park.

I'd dozed off every once in a while, then opened my eyes to stare up into that mysterious maze."

"It wasn't even a film," someone said, sounding bored.

"It was to *me*," I countered. "It's my very first memory, and I screen it every so often like a silent classic at a revival house."

"Did it have a plot?" asks another, as laughter ripples like a squall through the theatre.

"I suppose, but I've never been able to figure it out. It becomes more and more complex as I grow older."

"Who's in it?" asks a girl in a voice so soft it's like an echo from a seashell.

"There are so many characters it's impossible to keep track of them all."

"A cast of thousands!"

"Yes," I tell them, "and you're all in it!"

Laughter.

The soft-voiced girl says, "What genre is this? Is it a documentary?"

"It's a suspense film, I think, but there's comedy, too. It's a bit like real life."

I glance at my watch. I'm surprised by how late it is.

"I'm afraid I've run over my time, so I'd better wrap this up. I'll take one more question."

I can't see their faces, but I point randomly, as if I can.

"How does the film end?"

A sudden silence descends on the house; no murmurs, no shifting, no creaking of seats. It's eerie.

The lights begin to dim. I turn and step to my mark at center stage, turn slowly around to face them again. A single spotlight illuminates my figure and the darkness beyond is deep and impenetrable.

"You see, I haven't seen the ending yet. And neither has anyone else. So that's the one question none of us can answer. Not even the critics. All I can say is . . ." I pause for effect, a long moment.

"... I hope it's a happy one."

FADE OUT

AMBIGUITY FOR TWO
A One-Act Play

SCENE ONE

The exterior of a two-story corner building on a street in New Orleans which is named Elysian Fields and runs between the L & N tracks and the river. The section is poor but, unlike corresponding sections in other American cities, it has a raffish charm. The houses are mostly white frame, weathered gray, with rickety outside stairs and galleries and quaintly ornamented gables. This building contains two flats, upstairs and down. Faded white stairs ascend to the entrances of both.

No wait, that's all wrong. That's A Streetcar Named Desire. Sorry about that. Here, let's try this:

The interior of a two-story building on a street in San Francisco which is named Tunisian Fields and runs near the trolly tracks. The section is posh—one of the most expensive neighborhoods in America. The flat is sparsely decorated in a fashionably minimalist style. George (a man in his early 30s, well-dressed, exudes a raffish air) and Martha (a young woman, mid-twenties, his goth trophy wife with a tattoo on her left arm) sit facing each other across a sleek, industrial coffee table.

In the background, a framed photograph of Rrose Sélavy hangs on the wall. A bay window looks out onto the Golden Gate Bridge.

Intermittently, we hear a distant fog horn.

GEORGE: Well, here we are. Just the two of us.

MARTHA (*smiles*): I wouldn't be so sure of that.

GEORGE (*gives her a look*): I'll pretend I didn't hear that. (*Takes a deep breath.*) I think it's time we had a talk.

MARTHA: I was thinking that, too.

GEORGE: We think alike.

MARTHA: We do.

GEORGE: So . . . should I go first?

MARTHA: Does it matter? (*Smiles.*) Sorry. You first.

GEORGE: I'm not sure where to begin . . .

MARTHA: OK, I'll go first.

GEORGE: No, we agreed. I go first.

MARTHA: Ladies first.

GEORGE: Right. Now where was I?

Martha arches an eyebrow.

MARTHA: You were about to tell me what you've been meaning to tell me. Maybe you should just come right out and say it, and stop pussyfooting around.

GEORGE (*nodding*): Here it is then. Ever since I was a little boy . . .

MARTHA: Is this going to be one of your long stories? If so, maybe we should have lunch first.

GEORGE (*frowning*): Ever since I was a little boy . . . I knew I was a woman.

Martha stares at him for a moment, then begins to giggle.

GEORGE: What's so funny? Jesus, this isn't easy for me, you know.

MARTHA: Forgive me, George . . . it's just how you said it. It sounded silly. But I know exactly what you mean. I really do.

GEORGE (*surprised*): You do?

MARTHA: Ever since I was a little girl, I knew I was a boy. That's what I was going to tell you.

They stare at each other for a long moment. George rises, walks to the window and looks out.

GEORGE (*turns to face Martha*): That changes everything.

MARTHA: It does? Why?

GEORGE: Well, yes. I'm having a sex-change operation. So.

MARTHA: So am I.

GEORGE: You are?

MARTHA: I've been thinking about it for years, actually. But last weekend when we were at the opera . . . it all came together in my head, just like that. A no-brainer.

GEORGE (*nods knowingly*): I gave it a lot of thought, too. I made up my mind in New York. Remember that day we were walking along Fifth Avenue and I was staring at swimsuits in the window of Lord & Taylor's? . . . You practically had to drag me away.

MARTHA: Yes. I thought you were fixated on that manikin's boobs.

GEORGE: I was.

A long silence.

MARTHA: Oh.

GEORGE: Yes. I was wondering how I'd . . .

MARTHA: I *get* it.

GEORGE: Have you ever . . . ?

MARTHA: Just magazines. I subscribe to *GQ*.

GEORGE: I wondered about that.

MARTY: So what do we do now?

GEORGE: Go through with it, of course. Both of us.

MARTHA: But George, are you—

GEORGE: *Georgette*. Call me Georgette. You might as well get in the habit. What bout you? Have you picked out a name?

MARTHA: I can't make up my mind. It's a toss-up between Matt or Marty. Or does Marty sound too girly.

GEORGE: Marty is fine. I can see you as a Marty.

MARTHA: I could go in a completely different direction. What about Llewelyn?

GEORGE: God no! Nobody can spell it.

MARTHA: OK, George—Georgina—

GEORGE: Georgette!

MARTHA: Sorry, *Georgette*. I'll go with Marty.

GEORGE: Sounds good to me. Then that's settled. We're over the first hurdle.

MARTHA: That was the easy part.

SCENE TWO

One week later. Georgette and Marty are seated facing each other as in SCENE ONE, except they have switched chairs.

GEORGETTE: My appointment is tomorrow at four.

MARTY: How did you manage that?

GEORGETTE: I'm a lucky girl. Dr. Cooper is an old friend.

MARTY (*frowning*): Mine doesn't start until mid-September. There's a long waiting list.

GEORGETTE: I'll bet. Who's your surgeon?

MARTY: Henrietta Seggermann.

GEORGETTE: That's funny. I know a Dr. Henry Seggermann in Sausalito.

MARTY: That's *him*. I mean, that *was* him. He's a *she* now.

GEORGETTE (*smiles*): Small world.

Marty rises and walks over to the portrait of Rrose Sélavy. Cocks her head, trying to determine if the frame is crooked.

MARTY (*straightening the frame; over her shoulder*): There's something we haven't discussed.

Geogette picks up a copy of GQ from the coffee table and begins browsing.

GEORGETTE: What's that?

Marty returns to her chair and sits.

MARTY: Our marriage.

GEORGETTE (*puts the magazine down*): What about it?

MARTY: Have you thought it through? The rammifications. The kids. It's going to be hard on them.

GEORGETTE: Come on. Kids today, they multitask, they adapt to change so easily. Oh, sure, there will be a period of adjustment, but I wouldn't worry about it. They're teenagers. They've got their own problems.

MARTY: But will we be ... I mean, after the treatments and the name changes and everything ... will we still be *legally* married?

GEORGETTE (*easily*): I don't see why not. Just because you redo, say, the plumbing in your house, it's still the same house, right? *(Marty winces.)* Poor choice of words, but you know what I'm saying. What's changed, really? I mean other than, you know, this and that.

MARTY (*looking doubtful*): I suppose ...

GEORGETTE: Think of it this way, we're just closed for renovations. It's temporary. And in the meantime, it's still *us.* (*Smiles.*) The new us!

Marty considers this for a moment, then brightens.

MARTY: You're right! It'll be the same. (*Pauses, thinking again.*) Only different. But basically the same. We're still people. It's not like we're becoming aliens or something. We're still a couple. The only thing different will be the car.

GEORGETTE: The car?

MARTY: I'll be driving.

GEORGETTE: Oh. Right. That'll be a change.

MARTY: The most important thing is that we still love each other. Right?

GEORGETTE: I can only speak for myself, but . . . (*Reaches out and takes Marty's hand.*) I love you, Martha.

MARTY: And I love you, George.

They both cry "Oh!" and then begin to laugh.

CURTAIN

THEME PARK

Nothing beats a moonlit joyride down Sunset at 85 mph. Once I'm through the Strip and past Angelina's billboard boobs, it's clear sailing—full speed ahead. Top down, tires screaming, acing the curves on two wheels. I'm high on half a dozen day-old doughnuts from the remainder bin at Stan's. Eyes saucer-wide, adrenaline pumping, not a cop in sight. I experience a queasy—although not unpleasant—sensation in the pit of my stomach as the Jeep skateboards over a blind rise and tears downhill, whizzing toward the intersection, heading straight for the Pacific.

. . . But wait . . . Call right now and you'll get a second pair free! . . .

From an aerial view it would look like a suicide mission, but I hit the brakes at the last second, fishtail through the stop sign, and come to a whiplash stop in the middle of the highway.

I sit in shocked silence for a few seconds, stunned by this maneuver before I gun it again and banana-peel north toward Malibu.

Like Tante Verde, Sun Ridge Canyon is surrounded by mountainous desert terrain. But here the lush, green fairways sit upon the floor of the mountain canyons themselves.

Pepperdine appears like a ship stranded on a tall sand bar, but it isn't in view for long with the speedometer twitching around 96. Just a vanishing blip on the sonar. At this hour (almost 2 a.m.), the roadside holds few attractions, just the electric swell of the ocean.

. . . and her latest product line with the new Age Braker Serum and EyeFirmation Mask and Peel, which she herself guarantees will give you younger looking skin or your money back . . .

Oncoming headlights send a distress signal to my foot which slides intuitively off the accelerator. Normally I'd cannonball through the "Falling Rocks" zone—(nobody pays attention to those signs)—but headlights are another matter. Could be the CHP.

. . . Eight hours of moisturization, eight hours of free radical protection. And in the meantime, your expression lines are smoothing out. Melting away . . .

False Alarm. Just a pick-up with a load of shrink-wrapped matresses. Up ahead I spot a sign I've never seen: "Theme Park—1 mile."

On a ridge in the distance, a maze of twinkling lights appears like a foreign city in a dream. Everything is lit up in colors and a pair of spotlights sweep the sky. A kid is wagging a pair of flashlights at me and I skid off the road and nearly clip the bastard. He takes it in stride, though— gets up, dusts himself off, signals me forward.

"I'm OK," he says, like I care. He points to a roped-off area the size of a football field. It's as crowded as a Mercedez dealership in Abu Dhabi. "Plenty of free parking."

"You're open this late, huh?"

The kid grins. "24/7!"

I inch forward to where another attendant flags me into a space between two matching black SUVs.

. . . other sunglasses sell for one hundred, two hundred,

even three hundred dollars and they don't cut through glare and give you high definition color and clarity. Call and you can get our brand new HD Aviators for just ten dollars! . . . But wait . . . Call right now and you'll get a second pair for free! . . .

"Everything's free," the attendant volunteers. "Rides, booze, food, music." He lets out a whoop. "Even the girls!" He flashes me a thumbs up and struts off.

. . .Wicked indeed. And wickedly fun for those who love a challenge . . .

There has to be a catch. Nothing in L.A. is free, not even the block parties. I start walking up the dirt pathway lit with colored lanterns. I estimate ten minutes to reach the entrance but, hell, for free booze it's worth it. Besides, I can use the exercise.

. . . Still, sooner or later, you're gonna go astray. Don't forget to look up and enjoy the final three holes . . .

When I reach a neon archway flashing **WELCOME TO INFOWORLD**, a middle-aged bald guy on a stool looks up from his *Hollywood Reporter* and hands me an octagonal plastic tag with "I'm Tuned-In! (#1,418)" scrawled in marker.

"What's this?"

. . . Whether it's Botox or hyaluronic acid injections, sometimes the only thing more painful than the sting of the injection is the sting of the cost . . .

"Your lucky number," he says flatly. "If it buzzes and them little lights come on, you're a winner. Clip it to your shirt. Every half hour they announce a prize. Lady from Denmark just won a Thighmaster."

"There's no admission?"

He gives me a funny look. "Hey Mister Worry-wart, just go on in and enjoy yourself. The green gate on your left."

. . . If you've got this problem, we've got your solution: doctor-

recommended Beta Prostate. Beta Prostate is made with 13 natural ingredients that target your prostate. Imagine: quicker bathroom trips . . .

Through the green gate I go and suddenly two clowns—and I do mean clowns (red bulbs on their noses and big floppy shoes)—grab my arms and start hustling me toward a large tent. At first I thought it was a gag, but they were inordinately rough.

"Hey, what are you doing?!"

One jammed a long needle into my arm.

. . . better relief, and a full night's sleep . . .

∽

I open my eyes and the bright lights hurt. I have no idea how long I've been out. An hour? A week? I'm in some sort of amphitheater. I can make out a balcony with tiered seats high above, populated by distant, featureless figures.

A man in a white lab coat leans over and smiles.

"Ah, good, we're awake. I'm Dr. Valentine."

A cluster of words gather on the edge of my tongue, but it's a struggle to get them out.

"The clowns . . . where . . . what happened?"

"You're safe and sound now, Mr. . . ." The doctor consults his clipboard. ". . . Mr. Mattingly."

"*Where am I?*"

"You've had a successful operation."

My head is throbbing. I move my hand up to touch my scalp and feel a bandage.

"Don't worry. The scarring won't be visible once the hair grows back. I just need to run a quick test and then you'll be off on that well-earned vacation you've been dreaming about."

Vacation. The word reverberates in my head. I try to recall if I've ever dreamed about one. I can't.

A nurse appears at the doctor's side. She looks very familiar . . . pretty . . . an actress . . . I've seen her on TV, but I can't remember her name. Something with a vee . . . Vivien? . . . Valorie? . . . Vanessa? . . . And then it hits me.

"Aren't you Victoria Principal?"

She smiles vaguely, and turns to the doctor whose head zooms in close to mine, blocking her from view. He grins. "Right you are, Mr. Mattingly. Vicky is helping us out today, as everyone here at Infoworld wears many different hats. You'll be seeing a lot of Vicky in the future, as well as other world-famous celebrities, but now it's time for that little test . . . Vicky, if you'll take your position next to Mr. Mattingly here, we'll begin. Sid, can we lower the lights?"

The lights dim to near darkness, except for one amber beam illuminating the actress. She looks down at me. Her eyes seem unnaturally bright.

"Good afternoon, Mr. Mattingly. I'm Victoria Principal."

A thunderous applause erupts from the invisible audience. She does a cute little hand-puppet wave in response, then looks back at me.

"You probably know me as an actress from my many roles on stage and screen, but in recent years I've built one of the largest and most influential skincare companies in the world. Now I know you have some important questions for me, so fire away!"

My mouth springs open. I start to speak, but the words are *not* mine. They flow like a river and it's impossible to stop them.

"Yes, Victoria, there's a lot I'd like to know, so I'll cut to the chase. Most products today are aimed at Baby Boomers, but there are a lot of us thirty-somethings out there whose skin has been prematurely deteriorating due to Climate Change and the various toxins haunting our air. We look in the mirror and barely recognize ourselves. We'd like to know if there's

any chance our skin can look as young as it should. We've been living under power lines, atop toxic waste dumps, been bombarded with WiFi beams, consuming cancerous foods, and our faces are starting to show it—deep lines we didn't use to have, crow's feet, lesions, bloody blisters and a deathly grayish pallor. In your professional opinion, is there any hope for us?"

"Cut!" cries Dr. Valentine. "Excellent! Mr. Mattingly, that was flawless. I think we'll only need one more take. Vicky, if you'll pick it up from your next line. Quiet everyone. OK, cameras roll!"

"Why yes there is, Mr. Mattingly. You see, when I started my compamy, Principal's Principles, one of my goals was to erase *premature aging* from the face of the earth!"

Loud applause from the audience.

She nods at me. I stare up at her dumbfounded. She rolls her eyes.

Dr Valentine's voice: "Cut! . . . That's *your* cue, Mr. Mattingly. The word 'earth.' Here, let's try it again. On three, Vicky. One and a two and a three . . . "

She clears her throat.

"Why yes there is, Mr. Mattingly. You see, when I started my compamy, Principal's Principles, one of my goals was to erase premature aging from the face of the *earth*!"

Strange words escape my lips:

"Speaking of goals, Victoria, you once did something unheard of for an actress of your stature. It was so radical and it changed people's lives forever. You washed your face on national television!"

The audience cheers wildly.

Voices cry out: "*Amazing! I saw it! Bravo!*"

"Cut! That's a rap! . . . Mr. Mattingly, you've passed with flying colors! OK everybody, let's give him a round of applause for a superb performance!"

∽

I spent two weeks recuperating at Malibu Palms Resort. That's where everyone here at Infoworld is housed. I have a one-bedroom condo facing the ocean. There's a beautiful 9-hole golf course, 12 tennis courts, indoor and outdoor pools, a spa, cinema, three restaurants and a gourmet market.

And best of all, everything is *free.*

The studio is just a few blocks from my apartment. I'm fortunate to have been designated a full AP-Class 1. Audience Participant. It takes some people years to achieve that rank. And thanks to the operation, I never have to memorize my scripts; the implants take care of that. I have a short four-day work-week—Monday through Thursady, only three hours a day. The rest of the time is mine to do what I want.

We aren't allowed to the leave the community, but nobody wants to because we have everything we need right here.

Cars are not permitted at Malibu Palms. Everyone drives a golf cart. They don't go very fast, but that doesn't bother me at all. I don't have to worry anymore about those goddamn speeding tickets.

THE UNNAMABLE

HAFIZ on my way to the LONDON POST ORPHEUS to MAILER a LEVERTOV to MAUGHAM. As I PAZ through the PARKER, my BACH began AIKEN. I SATIE down on a nearby BENCHLEY, first MENCKEN SCHORER it was DREISER. An INGE of SNOW had fallen recently—HAILE REMARQUE-a-BÖLL for the MIDDLETON of JUNO— and there was a CRISP TRILLIN DE VRIES.

I SITWELL HUEFFER an AUERBACH ANOUIL set in. My throat felt DRYDEN, all NIETZSCHE, STRACHEY, and RAWLINGS.

"HEINE a CAPOTE," I told myself; however, I'd have settled for a GLASS of RILKE, some LEHMANN-ADE, or even a PEPYS-ZOLA.

LOWELL and behold, I spied a can of BEERBOHM LYONS in a PATCHEN of GRASS where the SNOW had been MILTON.

HECHT, it had been WRIGHT UNTERMEYER nose all the time!

Not bothering to MONTAIGNE my dignity, I bent down to PEAKE it UPHAM and—SHAW enough—discovered it was FULLER. I took a HARDY ZWEIG (SPILLANE some down my WESTCOTT) and found it FOWLES to my taste, like a GENET tonic spiked with SAKI. But HELLMAN, as my MUMFORD always told me, a BAKERs KANT be CHAUCERs.

When the BEERBOHM was ALGONQUIN, I DES-CARTES the empty can at my FOOTE. My head was SPI-NOZ A round and I had a CREASEY sensation that something was AMIS.

Was I being PARRA-noid?

IVANOV to LORCA round, to make SARTON I was ALONSO.

"I DUNSANY body . . ."

STILL I had the urge to RUNYON, as if pursued by a crazed VILLON—a *MUIR-DURAS!*

ANONYMOUS tell you I was truly a-FREUD for a WYLIE. But finally, when I felt a bit SAFIR, I returned to the BENCHLEY and was overcome by SARRAUTE. You see, I was VERDI POE; without ALGREN of SAND in my pocket. I GUEST EUCLID SAYERS I was the UNRUH-CHEEVER in my family. My BRODER OWEN DOYLE WELLS. My CICERO a CASTLE and had lots of CERVANTES, including a BUTLER, COOKE, and VALERY. Why she even had a maid to CERF her DINESEN bed!

I, of CORSO, was not USTINOV luxury. My wife and I lived in a rundown TOLSTOY BIGELOW without even a bloody BARTH-room. FERBER-MOORE, my wife was always accusing me of STEELE-LINDSAY MONET from her PERSE, and often threatened to THOREAU me out.

I COLETTE unfair, GODDEN-DURRENMATT all! WHAR-TON earth did she expect me to do? Rob FIRBANK?

I was on the VERGIL SOUSA-cide, just a HOPPER skip away from a ride in the HERSEY to the GRAVES-yard, when I was rescued by the sight of a PRIESTLY CUM-MINGS toward me. He held a DIDION Bible in one hand and a PARRISH-SAUL in the other.

It was a MERRICK-COLE!

"Beware of SETON, my son," WARREN the PRIEST-LEY, as if he were speaking from an invisible POHL-PITT. "O'NEILL down with me and pray. Time DOS PASSOS by and HAY-VENUS calling us. Repent before it's too LAYTON!'

Suddenly there was a loud KEROUAC of THURBER overhead.

"METERLINCK than never!" I cried, dropping to my knees just as the STORM hit—*POWYS!* It began raining KAZIN DODGSON HALE, too. Yet as soon as it had ASTARTE, it STOPPARD! And FROMM FLAUBERT the clouds came a beautiful RIMBAUD, and I saw APOLLI-NAIRE.

Was this the sign I had waited MOLIÈRE LONG FORD? I had to PYNCHON myself to see if I was dreaming . . .

༄

MALLARMÉ CLARKE WOUK me with a SARTRE. It ROUSSEAU loud I FALLADA my ALCOTT and received a WELTY on DEFOEhead.

Standing UPDIKE, HAZLIT a cigar and DE BEAU-VOIR filled with smoke. I began to KAFKA and moved to the OPPEN window for a breath of FRISCH EYRE. From BELLOW came the sound of my wife playing her ARP in her BAUDELAIRE, It sure was nice to HEARN she hadn't lost her PASTERNAK. MAUPASSANT I know could play as well as she.

I was suddenly HUNGERFORD affection, and I wanted to be near her now VIDAL my HARTE. Thus I made a SWIFT TROTSKY downstairs and HORACE across the HALL to her room. The DORÉ was a-JARRY so HYPERION-side and saw her looking STERN, HAGGARD, and (though I

HESSE-TATE to say it) rather STOUT. NOVALIS, she still looked PURDY good to me.

Upon entering the room, I spied two BOWLES of RICE SOUPALT on top of the PYE-ano.

"I see I'm AUSTIN time for BRECHT-FAUST."

My wife gave me a FROST-y stare. Don't BARTHELME,' she snapped, PUSHKIN aside her ARP. "You want to eat, AESOP to you."

VERMEEH presence SEDOV my WILDER desires. "May ICARUS you, my LAMB-CHOPIN? URIS lovely as ever."

"XAVIER breath."

I approached her CARR-fully.

"SABATINI kiss?"

"STEINBECK!" she warned. "You touch me and I'll call TALESE. They'll put you in BOURJAILY where you belong!"

"I'll swap you my pet BRACQUE BORGES JUAN kiss," I bartered. "It WORDSWORTH a BUCK or a POUND once."

She appeared skeptical.

"ORWELL, maybe just a penny, but—"

"You got CHAGALL! *Get out! Get out!*"

I made a GRABBE for he as she dashed for the DORÉ, and accidentally tore her ROBBE-GRILLET.

"EURIPIDES SAGAN I'm going to scream!"

I BELLOC her escape, PINDAR against the WALPOLE, and PROUST her to me.

Unfortunately for me, she drew a GUNN.

'NABAKOV!" she commanded. "I KANT STENDHAL your mushy LOVECRAFT!"

HIERONYMOUS admit I'd made a BOSCH of the situation.

"ISHERWOOD like to APOLLO-JOYCE for ACTON so WILDE," I told her. "I don't NOAH WAUGH CAMUS-VERNE me. But ALBEE good from now on, PROMETHEUS."

"I curse DAUDET EMMET you," she said, and spat. "JEFFERS think about *my* feelings? Of CORSO not, you

NIN-compoop. PICASSO you I missed my chance to marry that MARCEL-bound MARIËN-MANN from FRANCE. ALEICHEM. At least *he* knew how to earn a LIEBING!"

She sure knew how to hurt a GOYEN.

"Why, then," I asked, "did you DE SADE to MÉRIMÉE, HEMINGWAY?"

My wife frowned.

"You didn't ODETS then. Besides, I was JUNG, I liked your SOUTHERN accent . . ."

"Oh, BALZAC! It's because I was great in the SACK-VILLE. Admit it."

"Ha! HUGO look in the MIRO," she laughed. "You think you're DUCHAMP but, DADA, you're a LOOS-er."

"Well, then, IONESCO."

"That's right, GOGOL and BECKETT quick."

And so I left HOMER that afternoon and never saw my wife again. That was ten years ago. In a strange way, I think I still love her . . . yet, for the life of me, I can't remember her name.

GASLAMP

I was sitting in Your Alibi, a rundown hookah lounge on the fringe of the Quarter, staring blankly at a pair of talking heads on the screen above the bar. One head belonged to somebody with an obviously phony name—Reince Priebus. Since the sound was off I'd been trying to lip-read (". . . the *something* big government *something* have failed us . . ."), but it was giving me a migraine.

"Wassup, Tony?"

It was Lydia.

From out of nowhere she'd slinked up and was rubbing against me like a cat with an itch.

She had on her tight black *Psycho* dress with strategic slashes revealing shards of pale flesh. Her bare skin appeared to be winking in the dim lounge-light. Vampire black hair, flapper bangs, and a swash of pink streaks on the side. Petite and skinny as she was, Lydia had curves. She also had a nose-ring, pouty lips, Winehouse eyes, and a biker boyfriend in Chula Vista.

I motioned to the shifty-looking guy behind the counter and he shoved another Amstel at me. Lydia didn't drink. Her high came in capsules when nobody was looking.

I cracked a smile as I waited for the first non sequitur.

"Whose your favorite?" she said, as if our conversation from a week ago had still been in progress. "The Cramps, Gun Club, or Virgin Prunes?"

She was determined to convert me to goth, but like I told her, good luck with *that*.

"Can I have a week to think it over," I said.

Her nose-ring twitched.

"Nevermind." She frowned and scanned the room. There were a dozen or so amorphous patrons slouched on sofas or hunched over hookahs. This was not a place buzzing with energy; it was a way station prized for sheer inertia.

I met Lydia two years ago at a dance dive on University aptly named Apocalypse, because if the walls had ears they were all stone deaf. I had just come off a three-month sur-veillance gig in Rancho Penasquitos and was desperately in need of noise. Stake-outs are a one-way ticket to the looney bin. No one to talk to (Talk Radio doesn't count), you can't read a book. Coffee and trail mix is about as good as it gets.

She'd flown like a bat off the dance floor and latched onto my arm. "See the zombie over there—*don't look*—he's been *stalking* me all night."

I took her under my wing and we went outside for a smoke. She was speeding, so I got the Evelyn Woods version of her life story. Her dad was a Navy chaplain. They moved here from Minnesota when she was ten and lived in a station wagon out on The Strand. Her parents and an older brother, "Wolf" (now a Seal), bathed in the ocean and panhandled outside the Hotel Del on Coronado.

It was life on the precipice of paradise, until one day her dad found god.

A booming evangelical voice came over the radio and spoke directly to him. "I'm not shittin' you," she said, "it was just a crappy commercial." They drove to the nearest recruiting station and he enlisted in the Navy.

It was the start of a new life. They moved to an apartment in Barrio Logan where her father traded in his dream of owning a surf shop for a bible and a tat. It was the latter that inspired Lydia to get her own. Hers, however, didn't depict Jesus walking on water, but a Kundalini serpent licking her innie.

She had yanked up her shirt to show me, but when I innocently went to touch it, I got the *hands off, boyfriend* finger alert.

Seems we were destined to be a platonic odd couple: Goth Girl and Surveillance Guy.

Lydia worked downtown at a Kinkos, which was fortuitous. Whenever I needed enlargements for presentation in court, I took my photos to her. The first time she saw the pictures, she said: "These are totally *awesome.*"

That's not how most people would describe the grainy images, e.g., a couple leaving a motel at 3 a.m. or seen through the window of a Denny's. *Incriminating,* for sure, but not "awesome."

"You're a fucking artist, Tony."

I probably should have suspected something then, but the detective in me only functions when the meter's running.

A few weeks later, Lydia called and asked me to meet her at 3502 Adams for "a surprise." I was clueless. She assured me it was safe since Doak (her boyfriend) was out of town "on business."

I arrived at the address which turned out to be a used bookstore that had gone belly up. Lydia greeted me in black jeans and a Dead Kennedys T-shirt.

"Planning a break-in?" I said.

"No, we're going over there."

She took my arm and dragged me across Adams to a rundown one-storey with a sign over the entrance: Spaced Out.

One foot in the doorway, I got whacked with the surprise.

There, lining the walls, were a dozen huge blow-ups of my surveillance shots in silver frames.

Lydia grinned while I tried to catch my breath.

"Cheer up. You're gonna be famous."

She went and stood next to a photo of a prominent city council member getting a blowjob from a hooker. "This one's my favorite," she announced. "I couldn't think up a title. What do you want to call it?"

My palms were sweating and I felt like I might pass out.

"The end of my career," I said. "Call it that."

∽

Funny thing about San Diego on a Saturday night, there's this eerie silence that descends around nine, like everyone is waiting for the guest of honor at a surprise party. Then, by ten, it gets noisy like a weekend should, but at midnight it fades again to a deathly quiet.

Traffic on the 5 is light at that hour, the cars like penitent monks inching toward a monastery. Drivers hunched over speedometers with glassy-eyed intensity—high on pills and booze—eyeballing the needle, making sure it stays out of the red zone; praying they aren't weaving into someone else's lane.

Understandable, of course. If you're unlucky enough to get pulled over in this city, it's sweeps week and COPS is the only show in town.

Oh yeah, there are a few suicidal pencil-necks, tapping on their phones, texting their lives away, pedal to the floor. And there's always a batch of bloated Padres fans crammed into a monstro SUV with thumping Gangsta rap. Good old boys, hooting, slurring, and spitting into iPhones to their connections in Tijuana, or their pregnant girlfriends in Poway. Sometimes they wind up dazed and dumb-faced, standing on the shoulder beside a smoking metal hulk, or flat out in an ambulance headed to Sharpe.

Me, I never sweat it, since the only time I take my car is when I'm sober and working. Off-hours, I cab it.

Usually I call Betty since she's her own boss and craves the graveyard shift. Since we have smoking in common, she's always happy to see me.

For my part, I'm perfectly content to listen to her vent. She talks a blue-streak and I don't pay attention. All that's required is a "Right you are!" or "Ain't that the truth!" or maybe an exuberant "You tell 'em, Betty!"

All I know for sure is she's a lifelong Republican who hates the president.

Her lead-in is always the same: "Now you know me, Tony, I'm no racist, *but . . .*"

He was born in Zimbabwe or Kenya or someplace . . . hates America . . . is a closet homo, a member of the Communist Party, blah blah blah.

Like I said, I don't listen carefully because none of it makes sense, but there's still something comforting about her rants. We have a weird rapport . . . almost an intimacy. Maybe it's because we're both smokers and flout the law like Bonnie and Clyde. We roll down the windows and puff away like fiends on spring break. Sometimes, after a particularly conspiratorial rant, when she pulls up to my place, she'll wave away the bills in my hand and say, "Tonight's on me, Tony. Next week I'll charge ya double!"

Then comes an explosion—half laughter, half hacking cough—that rocks the cab like a Santa Ana.

"G'night, Betty . . . ha ha ha."

Inside my apartment on the second floor, I'll peer out the window and watch her perform her little ritual.

She gets out and pops the trunk, dons a pair of thick work gloves and a weird-looking Tyvek face mask, and rummages through a pile of chemical spray cans until she finds the right ones.

After a thorough interior spray-down, she has to wait 15-minutes before it's safe to get behind the wheel again.

"The fucking EPA banned this shit," she once confided. "I have to cross the border to get it, and let me tell ya, it *ain't* cheap."

I've invited her up a few times to wait, but she always refuses, preferring to stand on the sidewalk, watching the night sky and getting in a few extra smokes before her next fare.

According to Betty, we're the last two fuckers alive who still have the habit.

SIX RECIPES

1. Meat of the Sauce

The affectionate glower of the domicile habitué, the rare exalted passport of the lower, the colitis, clear attribute of the intelligence, the will to caress, to obsess over the sexist-manic-depressive, the will to desire a voluptuous cruet of the sexist-peseta, the maternal institute, the race-course-institute, the institute towards fetlock-worshipper, the institute towards artefact, towards nave, towards the ultimate mystery—all these thingamabobs have been called "love" that we should follow them and pursue them; all these brightly colored dildos have been called "love" yet we should avoid their flaccid allure.

2. Scent of the Frypan

The affectionate glow-worm of the dominance habitué, the rare exalted password of the loyalist, the collaboration, clear aubergine of the intensifier, the caress of the arsonist, the will to possess the sextant-manicure, the will to voluptuous cruise of the sextant-peso, the maternal institution, the racehorse-institution, the institution towards fetter-worth, the institution towards artery, towards navel, towards the ultimate mystery—all these thingummies have been called "love" that we should follow them and pursue them; all these sperm-worms have been called "love" and we must swat them away.

3. Lecher's Lychee

The affectionate glue of the dominion habitué, the rare exalted pasta of the loyalty, the collaborator, clear auction of the intensity platonist, the will to possibility of the sextet-manicurist, the will to voluptuous cruiser of the sextet-pessary, the maternal instruction, the racer-instruction, the instruction towards feud-wound, the instruction towards artichoke, towards navigator, towards the ultimate mystery—all these thinkers have been called "love" that we should follow them and pursue them; all these thinkers have been called "love" and we should smash their seductive reflections.

4. The Sausage Lynx

The affectionate glutton of vulva, the rare exalted pastel of the vaginal lubricant, the collapsed thighs, the clear-eyed audience ogling a threesome divided by two, the will to roast the sexuality-manifestation, the will to gnash the voluptuous crumble, smite the sexuality-pest, the maternal instrument, the sister-instrument, the instrument anointed with fez-frock comination, the articulation of ancient incest-bang theories on the ultimate mystery—all these think-tanks have been erected in the name of "love" but we should not follow them nor pursue the monsters of appetite; all these think-tanks have been called "love" but are merely trapdoors to corporate dungeons.

5. A Savage Sauté

The affectionate nosh of the donation, the rare exalted pastiche of the habitué, the monk's starched collar, clear audit of the interaction between savage and slave, the will to scribble a shack-manifesto, the will to devour the voluptuous crumbs of the pornographer's pesticide, the maternal instrumentalist, the lust-instrumentalist, the instrumentalist thrusting in loin-gasm, the instrumentalist inching towards artifice, towards purity, towards the ultimate mystery—all these thirsts have been called "love" that we should sip them; all these thirsts have been called "love" but are wanton metaphors drained of Eros.

6. Macaroons of the Seductress

The affectionate gnome guarding the shrink-wrapped casket, the rare exalted pastor of the lumberyank, the wooden colleague, the carved co-ed searching the auditorium for a seat at the orgy, the will to stroke in a sadistic shading-manner, the voluptuous crunch of the chomping rose, the maternal insurance, the racket-insurance, the insurance towards wife-wreck, the insurance towards artiste-o.d., towards neckerchief foreplay, towards the ultimate mystery—all these recipes have been called "love" but leave in a dream, vanishing from memory like a lover's long last shadow.

AND PORK PIES SAVE THE DAY
An Act of Terrorism Thwarted

Morning-room in Half-Moon Street. The room is luxuriously and artistically furnished. The sound of a piano is heard in the adjoining room. Each expletive is accompanied by a piano flourish.

ALFRED is arranging afternoon tea on the table as REGGIE enters.

ALFRED (*whispers*): Merdre.

REGGIE: I daresay there's some agro going on.

ALFRED: Get away! The troublemakers are all doing bird in Qwagsley.

REGGIE: Bloody hell! They didn't nab 'em all. And it only takes one duffer to plant explosives in a vase and Bob's your uncle!

ALFRED: Then Robert's your mother's brother.

REGGIE: Bollocks! (*Sneering.*) I think you've gone quite doolally.

There is a loud explosion in the distance.

REGGIE: Bugger that, I'm out of here!

ALFRED: Cheerio then.

REGGIE pauses at the door, tips his hat.

REGGIE: Chocks away!

ALFRED: Toodle-pip, old sport. (*Goes to the window, looks out.*) Hello, what's this?

REGGIE (*joining him at the window*): The wankers have arrived in time to save us!

ALFRED: Pork pies save the day—hooray! Curtain! Close the bloody curtain!

CURTAIN

IN A SEA OF SMARMY SWAMIS WHAT WAS HECUBA TO HIM?

When I was living in Los Angeles in the 1980s, I would go for a swim on weekends in that notorious sea of smarmy swamis off La Cienega. I'd drift past the squatters, the bearded bobble-heads hawking mantras in jam jars. "Just looking," I'd say, although I wasn't really looking, as my eyes were blinded by the blight. I had yet to discover my third eye, but that's another story.

Hecuba Davis was there with her sign: "Used Words, $1—Buy One, Get One Free."

I could never pass her by. You should see my collection— 6,326 words! That's more than some people have in their entire vocabulary.

My first acquisition was "plebiscite."

"This is pretty old, huh?"

Hecuba nodded. "It's an antique. 1860. From the Latin, *plebis scitum*."

"I don't think I've ever used it. I mean, not in a sentence. I've probably misspelled it."

"It's a tricky one," she said.

The words for sale were handwritten on 3×5 file cards which were stuffed in shoe boxes. Her tent was filled with tall stacks. There must have been a hundred boxes. The catch was you couldn't flip through the cards and pick a word you wanted. It was pure potluck. You reached in and plucked out a word. Sometimes you got a winner, sometimes a dud.

I keep *plebiscite* in a small gold frame above the TV. I store the others in a carton—each card in its own protective plastic sleeve, with a stick-on label, and a number. When I've acquired ten thousand, I'll put the collection up on eBay and make a tidy bundle.

Troy usually stops by when I'm shopping in Hecuba's tent. Last weekend, for instance. He always gives her a look like he wants her to finish up with me fast.

What was Hecuba to him or he to Hecuba? They weren't married (she wore no ring), but clearly they had a relationship. I've never seen them touch one another.

Troy has the assertive air of a pimp. He drives a red '57 Caddy convertible.

"How's it goin, Troy?" I say.

He doesn't look at me, just shrugs, leans his head out the tent flap and spits.

"I'll close up in a minute," she tells him. He grunts, mumbles something, and walks off.

She looks up at me with her big brown Bucks County eyes and smiles.

"Pick your free one."

I didn't know much about her, except that she relocated here from a town in Pennsylvania where her parents owned an antique shop. She grew up surrounded by Victorian furniture, German dolls, antique wedding gowns, and bric-a-brac. Whatever she touched had a price tag attached. "Everything in our house was for sale. Nothing was really ours."

Since childhood, Hecuba had a thing for words and devoured dictionaries the way some girls read romance novels. She'd always wanted to have a shop of her own, but had nothing to sell.

"One night I had this dream," she said. "I was in a strange city devastated by war. I was wandering barefoot through the ruins when I found a card buried in the rubble with the word 'hawk' written on it. It was like I'd found a bar of gold! The letters were glimmering. When I woke up, the idea for 'Used Words' was born!"

I'd always been tempted to ask how business was going. I never saw any other customers. Yet it seemed too personal a question, and there was this invisible barrier between us which I dared not breach.

I reached inside the box and plucked out a word.

. . . *inscrutable* . . .

"That's a good one," she assured me. "You never know when it'll come in handy."

"May I have a bag?"

She took the cards from my hand and placed them in a small brown bag. She smiled, said, "Don't Euripides," and handed me my words.

"I'll be careful."

"See you next weekend, Hector."

In the dream, both the king and his kingdom are destroyed. After she trips over Polyxena's corpse and finds Polydorus on the beach, she is driven mad by sorrow . . .

I can drift for hours in the *marché aux puces,* like a man on an inflatable raft in calm water. I ignore the music and eruption of voices surrounding me, oblivious even to the aromas emanating from the food trucks parked along the perimeter. The market itself seems as vast as an ocean and I imagine myself hundreds of miles from freeways, smog, SUVs, and chin-tucks. It is absurd, of course, since I'm smack in the center of the City of Angels.

There are unavoidable interruptions along the way. A

drunken brawl. Cops perp-walking a kid in handcuffs. When I come to the Tantric Yoga tent, I'll stop to sign a petition to legalize marijuana or free a political prisoner whose name I've never heard. I often wonder whether my signature makes a difference or if anyone even sees it. But it feels good to sign something.

Eventually I grow weary of wandering and head for the parking area. As I approach, I hear the ancient theme from *Jaws* in my head and spy two red fins gleaming in the sun. There sits Troy, in all his squalid glory, lounging behind the wheel, one arm draped over the passenger seat. He is revving the engine and thick toxic plumes mushroom up into the air.

The Caddy's tires begin to spin in a spray of gravel. As he peels out, the vanity license becomes visible: P-I-M-P-7, and Hecuba's head suddenly appears—her dark hair streaming like a pendant as the car squeals off down the street.

"Got a smoke, mister?" asks an old hippie in a t-shirt and black leather vest. His long gray hair hangs down to a Texas-sized belt buckle at his waist. He has a small skull tattooed on his forehead.

"Sorry, I don't smoke."

"Well then fuck you up the ass with a red-hot iron poker," he says, and chuckles.

I wished I had a comeback line, but I didn't. I never do. When he disappears in the crowd I think of shouting . . . *"Buzz off, you inscrutable old fart!"* . . . but it's too late and pretty lame.

When I find my Ford Festiva, I place the bag of words in the glove compartment, light a cigarette, and drive slowly back to my apartment in Tarzana.

∽

A few weeks later I was having my bagel breakfast while watching Eyewitness News. More fires, a couple of teen hikers were missing, and a bad car crash on the Ventura Freeway was holding up traffic. They had a sexy reporter live at the scene and when she appeared on camera she was applying some lip gloss. The anchor cleared his throat and said: "Uh, Christy, you're *live*." She looked flustered, smiled briefly, and grabbed her mic. In the background I could see an over-turned semi and underneath was a crushed red Caddy. The camera zoomed in closer so I could read the license plate.

Shit, it was Troy!

". . . *The truck driver was transported to Mercy Hospital with injuries that—according to the paramedic I spoke to moments ago—are not 'life-threatening.' The driver of the Cadillac was pronounced dead on the scene . . .*"

Did she mention any passengers? My head was spinning.

"*. . . because it was carrying hazardous waste that has spilled onto the roadway, the freeway will be closed for most of the day. Police are advising motorists attending the music festival to . . .*"

I jumped in my car and sped to the flea market. When I reached Hecuba's tent, I saw her sign and felt a twinge of relief, but when I stepped inside it was empty. All the boxes were gone—even her folding chair and table.

I ran to the adjacent jewelry stand where a woman in a bright orange sari was arranging her wares.

"Have you seen the girl over there who sells words?"

The woman made a face and pressed both hands to her cheeks. "Terrible," she said, shaking her head.

"*What happened?*"

"She was here early this morning when I set up. Some people came talk to her. She was screaming and crying and she run away."

"What happened to all her stuff?"

"Skinnies come . . . loot, take everything."

"Skinnies?"

She patted her head. "No hair, like . . . what you call them
. . . skin . . ."

"Skinheads?"

"Yes! They come in truck, take everything. I told them
stop but they laugh at me and one with big knife says he kill
me just like that. So I go hide in car. Real bad skinny man. I
feel very very sorry. She so nice, that girl."

I returned to the empty tent. It felt like a tomb. I stared at
the maze of shoe prints in the dirt. It resembled a mosaic. As
I turned to leave, I spotted a white card lying in the corner.

The bastards missed one.

I picked it up and there in Hecuba's inimitable script was
a word I'd never seen before.

barque

It looked like a typo, but knowing how careful Hecuba
was, I knew it had to have a definition.

When I exited the tent I heard the sound of a dog yapping
wildly. It was coming from inside the tent. I ducked back in
and looked around.

There was no dog and the barking stopped.

∽

I never saw Hecuba again after that. Funny how I hardly
ever think about her now.

Only when I hear a barking dog.

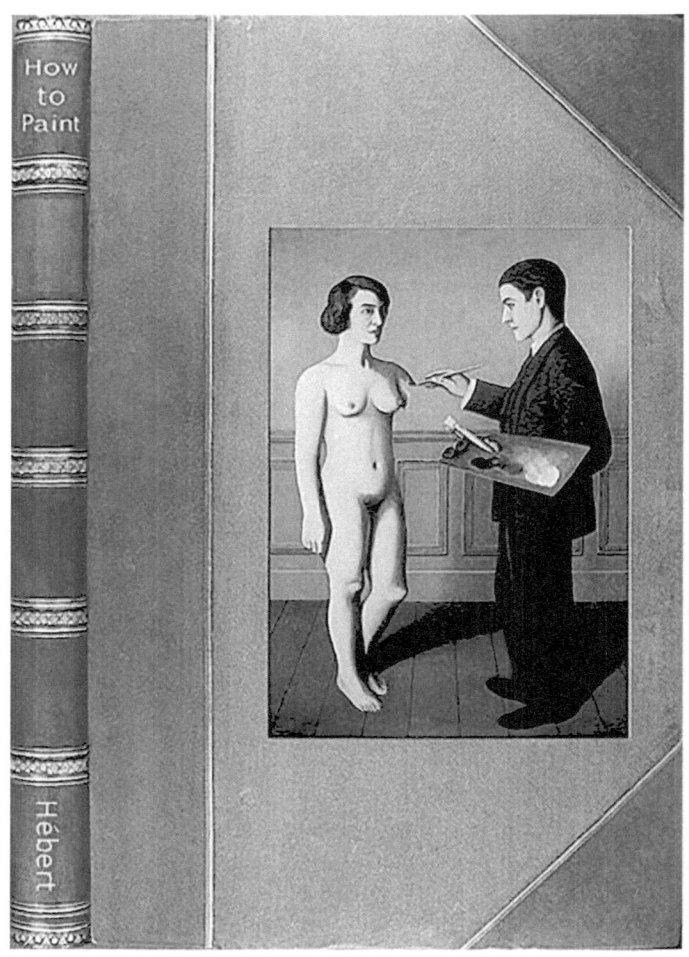

HOW TO PAINT

Originally published in France in 1930, *How to Paint* by Gustave Hébert is a very peculiar book. It is not a "how-to" by any means, for its author was a trained chemist and hack photographer, not a painter. The title, one eventually discovers, is an intentional misnomer—an ironic insult hurled at the Parisian art world.

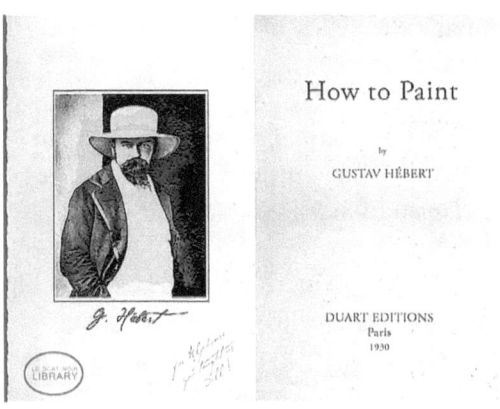

Released by the reputable house of Duart Editions, the original morocco-bound volume was financed by its author and designed in the elegant style of the 19th century. It was translated from the French by Hébert himself, and upon publication, caused a minor uproar. Although dismissed by critics as frivolous and absurd, the Paris Surrealists declared it a classic. In a review published in *Le Nouvel Oberservateur*, André Breton hailed it as "l'amour fou illuminé."

Adding to the book's mystique was a reproduction of Réne Magritte's painting, *Attempting the Impossible* (1928), which appeared on the front cover. In the absence of a subtitle, this was a cryptic clue to the nature of what was, in fact, a memoir. The title of a German edition (1967)—*Bein Malen, Versteckt Sich Man* ("When Painting, One Conceals Oneself")—is closer to the mark.

Hébert, the son of a chemist, was educated to follow in his father's footsteps, but abandoned science to pursue his true talent: chasing women. At the age of 19 he was given a camera and quickly realized the "opportunities" it afforded him. In 1921 he was hired as a photographer by the Paris-based Les Éditions d'Art Devambez, the largest publisher of lithographic post cards—those famously French risqué and pornographic relics marketed to tourists. Or, in the words of the author:

> ". . . *those pathetic souls who wandered the city like wraiths . . . glassy-eyed gentlemen from New York and London.*"

The firm's owner, Alfred Devambez, took a liking to the young man, and when he died three years later, Hébert found himself in charge of the lucrative enterprise. He devoted the next several years to seducing hundreds of models whom he photographed, amassing a small fortune, and collecting contemporary erotic paintings by artists such as Picasso and Delvaux. He became excessively concerned with the preservation of his collection and believed the paintings were fading prematurely. He wrote to Edmund Germer (the German inventor of the fluorescent lamp) seeking advice. Months later, Germer traveled to Paris to meet Hébert and agreed to collaborate on a series of experiments analyzing the effects of light on painted surfaces.

On November 18, 1926, they made a startling discovery. Using one of Germer's experimental arc lamps, Hébert coated its tube with a pyotized-fluorescing powder which transformed UV into an eerie, aqua-colored radiance. By shining the lamp directly on a canvas, which had been layered with a mixture of gouache and polynucleotide (a polymerase enzyme which causes pigments to erode), the light rays penetrated the opaque watercolors and, "in under a minute," exposed the blank surface beneath.

Although Germer found the effect "amusing," he was not particularly enthusiastic. Hébert, by contrast, was ecstatic.

"It fired my imagination—transported me to the base of Mount Helikon itself, where I stood in the shadow of the muses!"

He began referring mischievously to the discovery as "*pentimento-mori*" and considered using the pun as the title for his book but, eventually, ruled it out as too esoteric.

Inspired by a plan he believed would make him famous, Hébert selected twenty-six of his most explicit photographs, enlarged them, and glued each to a stretched canvas. He then enlisted the help of a painter friend whom he refers to only by the initials "M.C." (The artist was rumored to have been Marc Chagall.)

> "*At my direction he [M.C.] set about concealing the nudity in the pictures using the gouache mixture. With agile strokes of his brush, he clothed each model in suitably tasteful attire, using popular magazines*

> *as his guide. His génie artistique extended*
> *beyond painting over the offensive genital*
> *areas to include sartorial flourishes and*
> *embellishments such as hats, gloves, and*
> *jewelry. Working at a most feverish pace,*
> *he completed the entire series in three*
> *days!"*

Hébert spared no expense framing the painted photographs, and paid the esteemed Galerie sur la lune to sponsor an exhibition. Over 2,000 embossed invitations were mailed to members of Parisian society as well as government officials, foreign dignitaries, and stars of the cinema. Although no one had ever heard of the artist, on January 5, 1927, more than a thousand curious invitees showed up for the opening of Les habitants merveilleux de Paris: nouvelles peintures par Gustav Hébert. Since occupancy was limited to 200, many were forced to wait outside in a torrential winter rain.

Inside, visitors were greeted by a bizarre spectacle. Standing before each painting was a blindfolded attendant dressed in the uniform of a Victorian constable: a stovepipe hat, red swallow-tailed coat, white trousers, and Wellington boots.

With small groups gathered in front of each exhibit, the lights were extinguished and the gallery bathed in darkness.

A whistle blew, signaling the attendants who, one by one, switched on a small arc lamp attached to the painting's frame.

> "A rapt silence followed as the pedestrian paintings began to vanish under the queer illumination, and in their place appeared, as if by magic, my original photographs which lurked beneath the surface. The silence was broken by gasps. The ladies screamed, fainted, or fled. Fistfights broke out among the gentlemen. Curses and insults echoed like gunshots through the gallery. In short, my dignified guests went berserk."

From the sidelines, Hébert observed the scene calmly:

> ". . . Smoking a cigarette, I watched the ensuing pandemonium. The newspapers would be clamoring for interviews. My portrait would be caricatured on the front page of Le Scat Noir. Each photograph would be described in lurid detail. The exhibition would be the talk of the town!"

Finally, however, reality set in.

> ". . . my ebullience tempered by a dark cloud overhead. The authorities would be arriving soon. The festivities, alas, would reach their dénouement. I slipped out the rear exit and strolled off in the direction of home . . ."

The final chapter includes a photograph of the prison cell where the author wrote his book. The accompanying ten pages describe the cramped space in such minute detail that it anticipates Robbe-Grillet and the *nouveau roman*.

The book concludes with this quasi-poetic description of dust-motes:

> "... *tiny phantoms, souls of fleas, an animated composition rising from a tethered canvas, escaping by illuminated escalator to freedom—that pure, glittering realm of Eros—Eros everlasting. It is there (and only there) where one discovers how to paint.*"

SAD JAZZ AT THE FU MANCHU

The cats came from everywhere, crept, slinked, and oozed inside, found their seats without high-fives or yak. They were somber, funereal, hip to the core. There were whispers, of course, but no unexpected outbursts. They huddled at tables in the dusky lantern light. The poets had notebooks, the hustlers had phones, and there was an ambient electronic buzz in the air. Reminded me of summer nights in the country, crickets, the anticipation of something. There was always anticipation.

This was not that bookstore in North Beach. Nobody expected to hear "Howl" again, or Michael McClure roaring tantras at the moon. There might occasionally be the ghost of a Corso for comic relief, but no sad-eyed Kerouac bopping his chops, no willowy chick in black leotards chanting. The Beats were history now, textbook troubadours enshrined in a syllabus. The poets of this century were faux rockers, born-again punks and stand-up rapsters who did staccato like Vegas schtick. Maybe with a few dance moves thrown in, the hint of a moonwalk, a quick pirouette between adverbs—monotonous, minus the inspired monotony of *boxcars boxcars boxcars*. It made me long for a flicker of Patchen, the heart-felt, sonorous moan of a sax.

The stage was a small elevated platform just a foot high, but enough of a demarcation so nobody breached its invisible parameter. No fancy backdrop, a black cloth and the basics: speakers, a few stools, and mics clamped to C-stands. A pair of spotlights overhead. No gaudy disco strobes flashing shadows on the walls. Fu Manchu was no frills, bring your own attitude, and bring it they did.

The walls were covered in cloth, red and black, and each table had its own lantern hanging from a cord. The place wasn't Chinese (Bernstein, the owner, was Jewish), but it had an Oriental feel. The waitresses wore skirts with slits, high heels, and red halters. You had your choice of Thai beer or Turkish coffee. For food, there were bowls of mixed nuts, but no kitchen.

As for the name, Bernstein had intended to call the joint "Charlie Chan's," but opted for Fu Manchu because it had "more of an edge." He had planned for a jazz club, but then poetry sprang up spontaneously so every Wednesday night there were readings.

Tonight was supposed to have been music, but the quartet—(Pete Kincaid, piano; Buddy Rohmer, alto sax; Jamil Hendricks, bass; Clive Butler, drums)—would not be performing. Rohmer's career had come to an abrupt end— at the end of a knife, that is, in an alley off Pine.

No one had been arrested yet, but the cops were focusing on one Gisèle Honfleur, Buddy's French girlfriend who—as rumor had it—was maniacally jealous and given to fits of Gallic rage.

I was waiting for Inspector Maigret to show up. He'd flown in from Paris over the weekend at the request of the commissioner in Georgetown. Seems Mademoiselle Gisèle was over the bridge, barricaded in the French embassy, refusing to talk to the "American peegs." It was my job to provide the inspector with a bit of local color; show him around the neighborhood, give him a feel for the "mean streets."

We hadn't seen each other in ten years, so our first face-to-face had been devoted to nostalgia. The case remained firmly on the back-burner while we caught up. Why not? What was the urgency, nobody was going anywhere.

He'd conducted a brief interview with the suspect, who appeared distraught and claimed to have no knowledge of the crime.

"I examined her hand," he told me, "and I *knew* at once it was not the hand of a *keeler*."

Yeah, it made no sense to me either, but I wasn't about to question him as he was rarely, if ever, wrong. He wasn't a legend in France for nothing.

The clock on the wall said half-past ten. I turned toward the entrance and saw him leaning in the doorway. He motioned to me with his pipe. I drained the dregs of my mug and threw a few bills on the table.

Outside, it had begun to drizzle. The sidewalk glistened.

"Tonight is like a scene out of one of those novels, Jules," I said, turning up my collar.

He nodded and lit his pipe. The smoke hung in the air for a moment and I couldn't see his eyes.

"I'm pleased to report the murder has been solved." He smiled slightly, without a trace of irony. "I have—how do they say?—*cracked the case.*"

"Surely you're joking . . ."

"It was not all that complicated, mon ami. It never is. Especially when one is dealing with jazz musicians, n'est–ce pas? They improvise and one needs only follow their notes and the clues all appear."

"It wasn't the girl?"

"No-no, not Mademoiselle Gisèle," he said. "But she is not the *spectateur innocent*, either. She is implicated in a most banal *crime passionnel*. She was in love with the sax player, true . . . but she loved another even more fervently."

He paused for effect, his pipe having conveniently gone out, and made quite a show of relighting it.

"She was having an affair with the murderer," he said. "And it was *he* who lost control and stabbed Monsieur Rohmer in a jealous rage."

"But how did you solve it? A confession?"

Maigret waved his hand dismissively. "I received a copy of the autopsy report. It was all in there, as plain as day." He smiled vaguely. "The pattern of wounds gave him away. It was a pattern only a drummer would make."

He glanced at his watch. "Ah, mon ami, I'm sorry, but I must be off or I will miss my flight. This is no life! I come and I go and I sniff around."

He shook my hand briskly and climbed into a waiting cab. "We must get together in Paris next time."

"But wait . . . it was Clive the drummer?" I asked.

As the cab pulled away, Maigret leaned out the window.

"Oui," he said, "Monsieur Butler did it."

A STREETCAR NAMED GRUYÈRE
A One Act Play on Curds

Characters: JACK, *a young, atrociously handsome, hearing-impaired gigolo, and* BRIE DE MEAUX, *an aging film star and meth-addict.*

The Scene: New Orleans. A spacious bedroom on Bleu de Bresse Street. BRIE is seated at her dressing table, applying a third layer of make-up. JACK, her lover, lounges bare-chested on the four-poster bed in a pair of designer jeans. He is browsing through a copy of The Hollywood Reporter.

BRIE (*to herself*): Jesus . . . I look like something the cat on a hot tin roof dragged in.

JACK (*distracted*): Did you say cheeses?

BRIE (*frowning*): I said Jesus, your lord and savior.

JACK: Oh, I thought you said "cheeses."

BRIE: Jack darling, would you mind getting up and opening the window? The air is absolutely fetid.

JACK: Feta? Is it lunch time? Let's go to Mario's instead. They have that sublime Reggiano. Besides, it's your turn to treat.

BRIE (*laughs bitterly*): It's always my turn to treat. But not anymore, Jack. While you were getting your beauty sleep, the bank called.

JACK: Hank? Who's Hank?

BRIE (*shouting*): Bank, goddamit! (*Composes herself.*) I'm five hundred dollars overdrawn. By any chance did little Jack go shopping Saturday?

JACK (*long pause, thinking*): Oh . . . yes, I bought a suit. You can't expect me to walk around naked all the time.

BRIE: I don't think you heard me, Jack. I'm busted. Do you understand?

JACK (*grinning*): I love your boobs. You're built like a brick shithouse.

BRIE (*glaring*): I'm flat now, Jack. Dead broke.

JACK: What? Really? Cleaned out? (*Brie nods.*) So cash in your stocks and bonds.

BRIE: I already did that, remember? Suddenly last summer in Palm Beach, you wanted that little red Alfa Romeo.

JACK: It's not Alfa Romano . . . it's Pecorino Romano that I like. (*He gets out of bed, crosses to the closet and puts on a shirt, khaki pants and penny loafers. He packs a small suitcase.*)

BRIE: Where are you going?

JACK: Back to Monterey.

BRIE: But you can't go home again, Jack. You'll die of boredom in a week on that farm. (*Smiles.*) You weren't cut out to raise goats.

JACK: I'll talk Uncle Bud into giving me a small business loan. (*Turns and stares out the window for a long moment.*) I've always wanted to have a little shop of my own. Now's the time to make that dream come true.

BRIE: A shopkeeper? Good luck with that. What on earth will you sell? I mean, besides that gorgeous body of yours.

JACK (*picks up the suitcase, crosses to the door, pauses and turns to look at her*): Cheese, Brie. A little cheese shop. Very high end, only the finest imported cheeses. It's a guaranteed winner. (*Grins.*) Everyone loves cheese.

He exits. Brie shrugs, stares at her reflection in the mirror as the lights begin to dim.

CURTAIN

from WIFFLEDOWN WAY
A Sunny Novel Fraught with Dread

I shan't forget the summer I spent at Wiffledown Way. It was truly unforgettable, as it was only a few short weeks ago. Actually just one, to be precise, although I caution you not to expect any further precision as we proceed. I had just come down from Oxford, having completed my studies, and was sorely in need of *détournement dévergondée*. I use the word "studies" loosely, for the knowledge I'd acquired could fit inside a thimble with room to spare. And speaking of spare rooms, I'd taken one at the Stumble Inn, a cozy seaside Victorian on Lillywait Lane. This historic two-storey features a widow's walk at each end and is situated between a pair of stately, homoerotic elms. From a distance, the structure resembles a coat of arms.

It was a tad early in the season, so the only other occupant of this shady abode was one Priscilla Pemburton. Yes, *that* Priscilla Pemburton—Sir Henny Pemburton's niece. A lovely girl, pale as sand, with amber windblown hair, bright periwinkle eyes, and a figure able to stop traffic in Trafalgar during a dirty bomb attack.

Alas, Priscilla was recovering from an ill-fated affair with that venomous rake Reggie Ventwhistle. He had broken the engagement on the eve of their wedding. Good timing, what? The sheer gall of the lout was enough to make me see red—no small achievement since I'm legally colour blind. But that's neither here nor there, most likely somewhere in between. I met this sad-eyed damsel under rather unfortunate circumstances. However, let us step back a few paces here while I present the facts in their natural order, although the word "natural" is quite inappropriate.

The morning had started off admirably for, upon awakening, I experienced a glowing sense of well-being which did not diminish with the passage of breakfast. Indeed, it seemed to increase as the minutes crawled on. So full of effervescing energy was I that, departing from my customary late-morning nap, I picked up my hat, stuck it at a rakish angle on the old bean, and sallied forth on a healthy tramp to the village green.

It was while returning, flushed and rosy, that I observed a sight which is rare in England: the spectacle of a bishop, armed with an AK-47, shooting into a crowd of well-wishers. It is not often in a place like Wiffledown that one sees a bishop at all, let alone one committing mass murder. What struck me at the time as particularly odd were his high-pitched cries of "Allahu Akbar!! Allahu Akbar!!" as he blasted away into the screaming throng. I knew not what those strange words meant, but a subsequent visit to the little library on Sea Froth informed me the expression was Arabic for "God is great" or, to be precise, "God is greater."

I daresay I made it back to the rooming house in a jiffy— as if I'd been shot out of a canon—and who should I stumbled upon seated on the veranda but the jilted Miss Pemburton in the flesh! Shoulders slumped, head in hands, she was, in short, a train wreck.

Well, they don't call me Booster Wister for nothing. I fairly sprang into action.

"I say," I said, "what seems to be the trouble? Such a ducky day. Right ho! Aren't you Priscilla Pemburton, Sir Henny's niece?"

She looked up and smiled faintly. "Why yes . . . yes I am."

"Pleased to meet you, I'm Artie Wister—Booster to my chums." I took her pale hand in mine and gave it a gentle rattle. "Why so glum on such a sunlit day?"

"You haven't heard the news then?" she said, suddenly wide-eyed. "An ISIS-sympathizer murdered thirteen people in cold blood!"

"Go on! Thirteen? Why that's a baker's dozen. Bloody awful!" I removed my hat and scratched the old nut. "Funnily enough, on my way back here from my morning walk, I spotted a bishop shooting into a crowd, but surely it's unrelated. I mean, a bishop, after all."

"No-no," she cried, "that's him! That's the terrorist! Bishop McFarley from Brighton. They say he pledged allegiance to al-Baghdadi on Facebook this morning." She shuddered. "It's so frightfully dreadful."

I couldn't deny it; Facebook had devolved into an uncivilized network of barbarians—most of whom are devoid of social graces, prone to the most egregious typos, and who never even bothered to "like" my clever postings. Thus, last year, I deactivated my dashed account, and bid good riddance to that den of narcissistic nitwits and their selfies!

I flashed Priscilla my winning everything's-going-to-be-hunky-dory smile and piped: "How about a stroll along the beach? The brisk salt air will work wonders on the glooms."

She looked at me askance for an instant with those sublime periwinkle eyes. Then came a discreet little nod. "I suppose you're right, Mr Blist—er—"

"Wister," smiled I. "Booster Wister."

"Oh, sorry." She let out a laugh, but quickly regained her composure and nodded. "I think you're quite right, Mister

Wister. No sense sitting around here moping."

"Precisely! Come along then. And please, call me Booster."

∽

"I say, Heeves, might you draw me a bath?"

"I might, sir. Which would your prefer, pen or ink?"

I winced. Heeves was my gentleman's gentleman and a man whose keen intuition and intelligence I greatly admired. However, it was his sense of humor I could do without.

"I surmise you'll be attending the Bafflemyte's dinner party this evening, sir?"

"That indeed is my intention, Heeves, and I'll require your splendid service behind the wheel at, say, sevenish?"

"Very good, sir. Sevenish on the nose." He nodded sharply. "I shall go and draw your bath now, sir, unless you'd prefer I stand here a bit longer looking peevish."

"No, no, just the bath, Heeves, that will be all, thank you, just the bloody bath. And no newts in there this time!"

He turned on his heels and oozed away.

I was looking forward to seeing Priscilla at the party, although I feared there might be a few obstacles I'd have to overcome. Namely, Sir Henry Bafflemyte who—how shall I put it?—detested me. To make matters worse, it was no secret in Wiffledown that he kept a lascivious eye on Miss Pemburton.

So why, you ask, was I invited? Fair question. And to be perfectly candid, there wouldn't be much of a story here if I simply lay about in bed playing with myself, now would it.

I glanced at the clock on the wall and calculated I had two hours to spare. Plenty of time for the drugs to kick in.

CORN ON MACABRE

I start my day with flapjacks, cognac and wisecracks. A stop and chat over at the deacon's flat. After a few slaps on the back, we count our blessings, this and that. His name is Max and he has a tendency to wax poetic (don't we all), but I've learned to steer him onto the fast-track. So off we go to trap rats in the sacristy, don funny hats and play craps. By ten, it's time for my mid-morning skin wrap, followed by a brief gap and a dip in the sap-vat.

Lunch is a picnic by the palms: mushroom caps and left-over slabs and scraps. Then a dash to the clinic for a stash-bath to keep my bristle-whiffer looking snazzy. I take an herbal soak-'n-choke, and then go snob-hopping down Rodeo. I stop to shop at Becky's Bootery, Flip-flops & Stilettos. I spy spats and taps, natch, and decide to song and dance my way over to Dada's Café for a frappe and a clap and flap. An hour of vaudeville, corn on macabre.

The afternoon is devoted to catnaps, flashbacks, and a brisk walk up the steampunk'd path to the grand Theatre Sarcey for a backstage tour of the flats and wings. Snags and traps abound, and it's a tricky two-step along the narrow catwalk above the fly loft. I catch a gaggle of flappers down below, clattering across the stage like they're dodging bullets.

I'm tempted to let loose a fistful of trolls with parachutes, like the final performance of *Fiorello* so long, long ago.

Before you or I know it, I'm backtracking down the proverbial spiral staircase, lunging for the omnipotent fire escape, scampering, sliding and landing with a thud on the lid of a dumpster. Ahh, but what's that sound I hear? A clapper? . . . The sweet clang of the dinner bell!

"My, how time flies," I muse, whilst ducking into a phone booth and donning a sappy-looking blue tux with crenelated cummerbund and back-snaps. Button up for safety, it's Potluck Wednesday at Frida's Galleria and you never know what you'll find on the menu.

CORN ON MACABRE & OTHER CONUNDRUMS

About the Author. The process of recording the events and circumstances of Norman Conquest's life, esp. for publication (latterly in any of various written, recorded or visual media); the documenting of Norman Conquest's life history (and, later, other forms of thematic historical narrative), considered as a genre of writing or social history. Sometimes with defining word, as critical biography, literary biography, political biography, etc. See also autobiography (n.), photo-biography (n.).

A written account of the life of Norman Conquest; (also) a brief profile of Norman Conquest's life or work. Later more generally: a themed narrative history of Norman Conquest in any of various written, recorded, or visual media.

Personal history; the events or circumstances of Norman Conquest's life, viewed collectively. Also: the course of Norman Conquest's life, or the life cycle of an animal or plant.

OTHER ANTI-OEDIPAL TITLES

Germany: A Science Fiction • LAURENCE A. RICKELS

In *I Think I Am: Philip K. Dick*, Laurence A. Rickels investigated the renowned science fiction author's collected work by way of its relationship to the concept and condition of schizophrenia. In *Germany: A Science Fiction*, he focuses on psychopathy as the undeclared diagnosis implied in flunking the empathy test. The switch from psychosis to psychopathy as an organizing limit opens the prospect of a genealogy of the Cold War era, which Rickels begins by examining Dick's *The Simulacra* and follows out with readings of *Simulacron 3*, *Fahrenheit 451*, *The Day of the Triffids*, *This Island Earth* and *Gravity's Rainbow*. This study addresses the syndications of the missing era in the SF mainstream, the phantasmagoria of its returns, and the extent of the integration of all the above since some point in the 1980s.

Induced Coma • HAROLD JAFFE

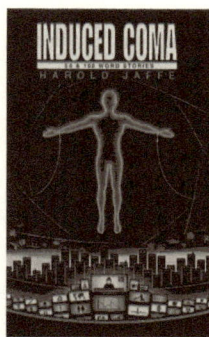

A semi-sequel to the visionary *Anti-Twitter: 150 50-Word Stories*, *Induced Coma: 50 & 100 Word Stories* once again features Harold Jaffe writing to the Nth power, taking as his subject no less than the benighted globe. Including published mainstream narratives and "news" articles from the US and abroad, the collection covers an extraordinary range of subjects—activist art, global warming, revolution, the entertainment industry, and the freakishly banal happenings of our day-to-day lives—all of which the author deconstructs to expose their ideological subtexts in uncanny ways. Satirical, critical, tragic and ruminative, Jaffe works every register and creates a bricolage in *Induced Coma* that turns mass media inside-out, all niceties stripped away.

Galaxies • BARRY N. MALZBERG

Metafictional, existential and sardonic, *Galaxies* is a masterwork of the Malzberg canon. The novel mounts a concerted attack against the market forces that prescribed SF of the 1970s and continue to prescribe it today. At the same time, the book tells a story of technology and cyborgs, of bureaucracy and tachyons, of love and hate and sadness . . . Despite his deviant literary antics, Malzberg could not be ignored by the SF community, winning the first annual John W. Campbell Memorial Award and receiving nominations for numerous other accolades in the genre. Nonetheless his writing has not received the attention it so profoundly deserves. *Galaxies* is among the works listed in acclaimed SF editor David Pringle's *Science Fiction: The 100 Best Novels*, published in 1985. With this new edition, Anti-Oedipus Press is proud to usher Malzberg's genius into the twenty-first century.

WWW.ANTI-OEDIPUSPRESS.COM

www.ingramcontent.com/pod-product-compliance
Lightning Source LLC
Chambersburg PA
CBHW020627130626
46552CB00003B/1112

* 9 7 8 0 9 9 0 5 7 3 3 2 6 *